Holy jumping quarks!

After all the commotion surrounding the first four issues of *Phantastique*, I thought a holiday was in order. Just a few null jumps through Sargos Space and I was on the wild and untamed world of Nemesis.

I swear it was only a two week trip. Didn't figure it being over 30 years back on Earth!

So the magazine had been put into stasis while I was gone.

Well, I'm back, so let's dust this sucker off!

The first four issues were pumped out between 1985 and 1986, and the fifth issue was all planned out but rummaging through the archives I've only found some of it.

So here I present some tales, some old, some new, all original! And in full ***bloody*** colour, too! That's an advancement.

I hunted down **Steve Carter** to reprise his role as Creative Director, and welcomed **Antoinette Rydyr** as Art Director, replacing **Dez Waterman**.

A huge thanks to **Rod Williams** for the superb cover illustration on this auspicious issue. The title was redesigned by **Steve Carter** with assistance from **Antoinette Rydyr** and **Ross Radiation** who wrestled it into shape.

A new addition to the crew is **Pete Correy** who provided his production and layout expertise. And special thanks goes to **Antoinette Rydyr** who provided most of the colouring and lettering for this resurrection issue. In fact, doing all that work has driven her completely crazy so we had to strap her into a straitjacket and bundle her off to the insane asylum.

The aim of ***Phantastique*** is to present weird horror, science-fiction and surrealist fantasy in the form of wild and vivid voyages of the imagination. The weirder the better, especially when there's a thread of eccentric internal logic holding it all together.

Horror, science fiction and fantasy are universal genres that transcend all ages, gender and cultural backgrounds. We prefer to focus on fantastical stories with universal appeal rather than limiting them to the parochial and the mundane.

We're not including any serials because we know how frustrating it is waiting for the next chapter, so all the stories are self-contained. And despite the controversy back when the first four issues came out, we will not shy away from depicting garish and gruesome gore. And we promise, no superheroes; there're way too many of them already!

This volume showcases an interstellar cast of artistic Australian talent including: **Steve Carter, Antoinette Rydyr, Rod Williams, Pete Correy, Dez Waterman, Dillon Naylor, Ross Radiation, Ryan Vella, Glenn Smith, Glenn Lumsden, Jason Paulos** and the enigmatic **Fred Enroht**.

So without further ado I present Volume 1 of ***Phantastique — Tales of Taboo Terror***.

Hope you enjoy it!

James Kronol, Editor.

P.S. For the story behind *Phantastique* visit: http://www.weirdwildart.com/words/phantasq.html

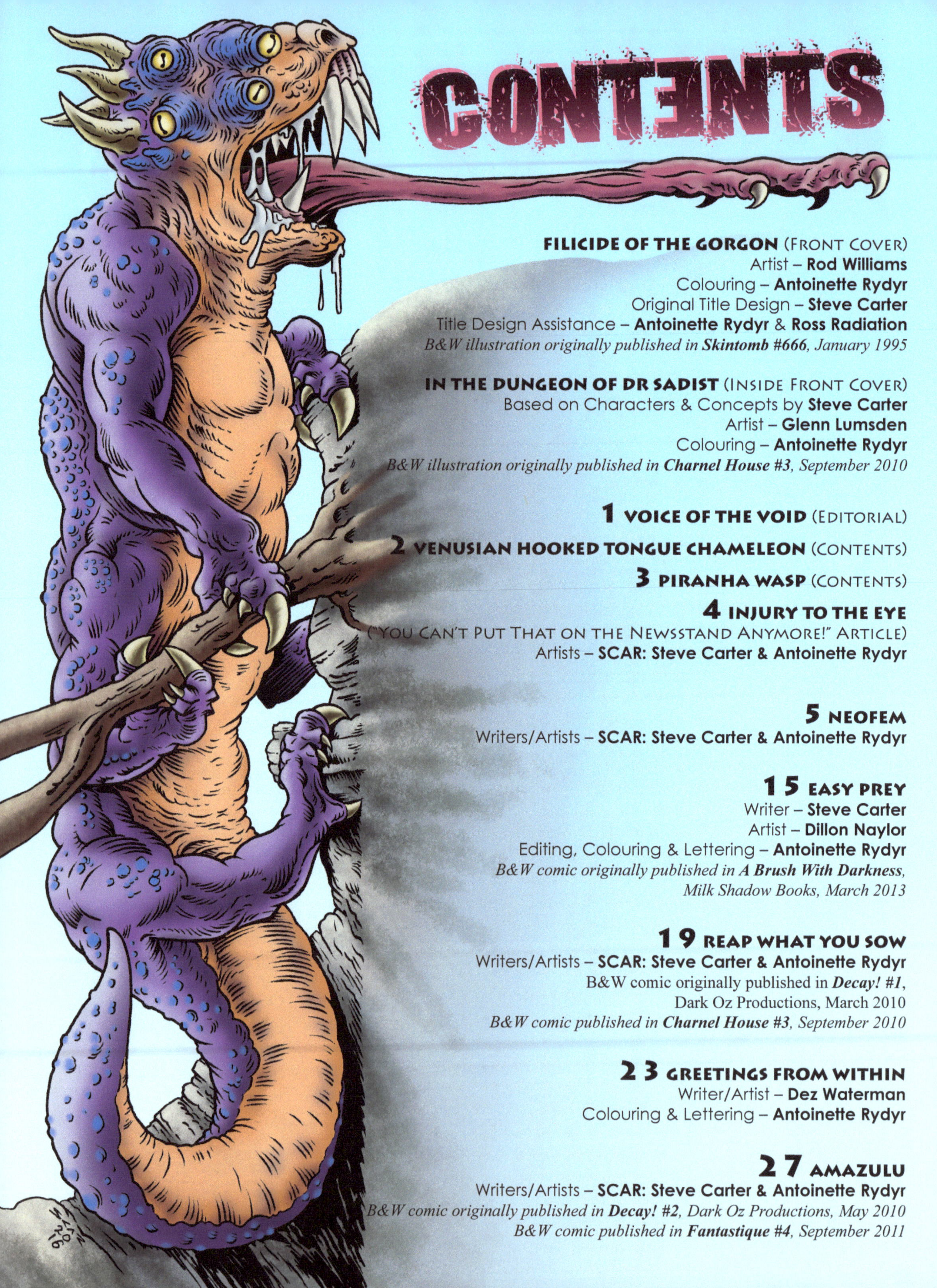

CONTENTS

YOU CAN'T PUT THAT ON THE NEWSSTAND ANYMORE!

Shortly before becoming involved with, and creating **Phantastique**, along with Frank Maconochie *(Financial Manager)* and Des Waterman *(Art Director & Production Manager)* in the early 1980s, I had just discovered the existence of EC comics and the furore over the notorious American horror and crime comics of the 1940s and early 1950s. It was then that I learned of Dr Fredric Wertham's campaign, which resulted in the implementation of the *Comics Code Authority* and ultimately crippled the entire comic book industry at that time.

One of a vast litany of offensive images found within these comics that Dr. Wertham fiercely objected to was what he referred to as the *"injury to the eye"* motif. When it came to creating the image for the cover of Phantastique #3, I simply couldn't resist the temptation and created a blatant visual homage to this "motif".

To my dismay, various colleagues and contributors vehemently objected to the illustration and persistently demanded that it be shelved. After much futile debate, I relented and, with a deadline looming, worked on a new idea for the cover of issue #3 -- the infamous and I believe, more original *"Now to Inject You With Our Sperms"* illustration. The final illustration was in fact created by myself and another very talented artist, Rod Denson.

The naysayers again firmly objected to the image, citing that it will never be allowed on the newsstand. They found it even more offensive than the previous "injury to the eye" image! At this point, I was through with debating the issue. There simply wasn't enough time. As it was, their fears were completely unfounded, and Phantastique #3 appeared on the newsagents' shelves in Australia. Sales were extremely good.

Needless to say, you can't put **that** on the newsstand shelf any more …or can you?!

Steve Carter,
Creator and Creative Director of Phantastique, a.k.a. Horror Phantastique.

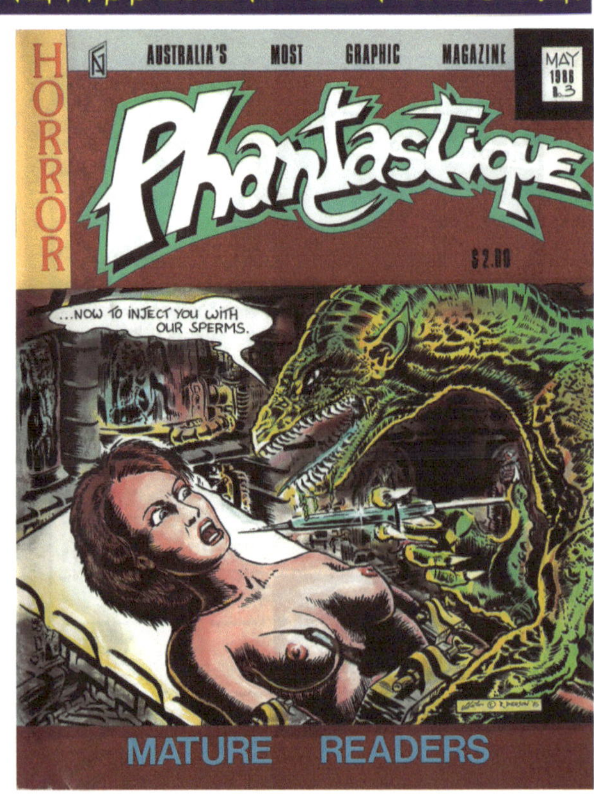

IT'S A LOST NEW WORLD! THE DESIGNER DRUG FEMJOLT GIVES WOMEN WHAT NATURAL EVOLUTION HAS NOT. IT TRANSFORMS THEM INTO GLAMOROUS SUPERWOMEN, GODDESSES WITH SUPERIOR STRENGTH. BUT PERFECTION COMES WITH DIRE CONSEQUENCES – AN INHERENT, HYPER-PREDATORY NATURE; FERAL, RUTHLESS, DOMINANT. RETROX, AN IMPURE STRAIN OF FEMFOLT, HAS BIZARRE, UNPREDICTABLE EFFECTS. BOTH SUBSTANCES ARE ADDICTIVE, AND WOMEN AND GIRLS WHO ARE TRANSFORMED BY THESE DRUGS ARE KNOWN AS. . .
NEOFEMS
BY SCAR © 2013
BECAUSE OF THE Y CHROMOSOME FEMJOLT AND RETROX HAVE A DIFFERENT EFFECT ON MALES.
FEMJOLT CAUSES A DISORIENTED, PSYCHOTROPIC "HIGH". LONG-TERM USERS DEVELOP A FORM OF CHRONIC DEMENTIA. CONTINUOUS USE OF RETROX CAUSES PROFOUND RETARDATION, DYSFUNCTIONAL SEXUAL BEHAVIOUR AND PHYSICAL DEFORMITY.
IAN STANLEY, UP-STANDIN' CITIZEN AN' EDITOR OF THE LOCAL RAG!
'E'S REAL VOCAL 'BOUT US, GIRL! BIN READIN' 'IS WEEKLY COLUMN!
WHINES ON AN' ON – SEZ ALL GIRLS AN' WIMMIN LIKE US 'R' MAD MURD'RUS MUTANTS.
DIDN'T THINK WE BOVVERED TA READ IT, DID YOU?
WELL, WE KNOW ALL 'BOUT CHA!
SURE DO. YER CRAP'S ALL OVVAH THA NET.
RANTIN' REFORMIST 'N' DO-GOODER'S A FRIEND OF SATAN'S GESTAPO!
HUH, YEAH! HYPOCRITE!
HIRED 'EM TA COME TU OUR TOWN 'N' GET RID OF US!
FOOL BOY – CROSSED THA LINE THERE . . .
TIME YA SHRUNKEN 'ED ADORNED ME GIRDLE BOY!
NO! PLEASE! LISTEN! SATAN'S GESTAPO? I HAD NOTHING TO DO WITH THAT . . . – BUT I KNOW THINGS ––
THEN YA BEDDA SPILL YA GUTS FAST – OR WE'LL SPILL 'EM FOR YA!

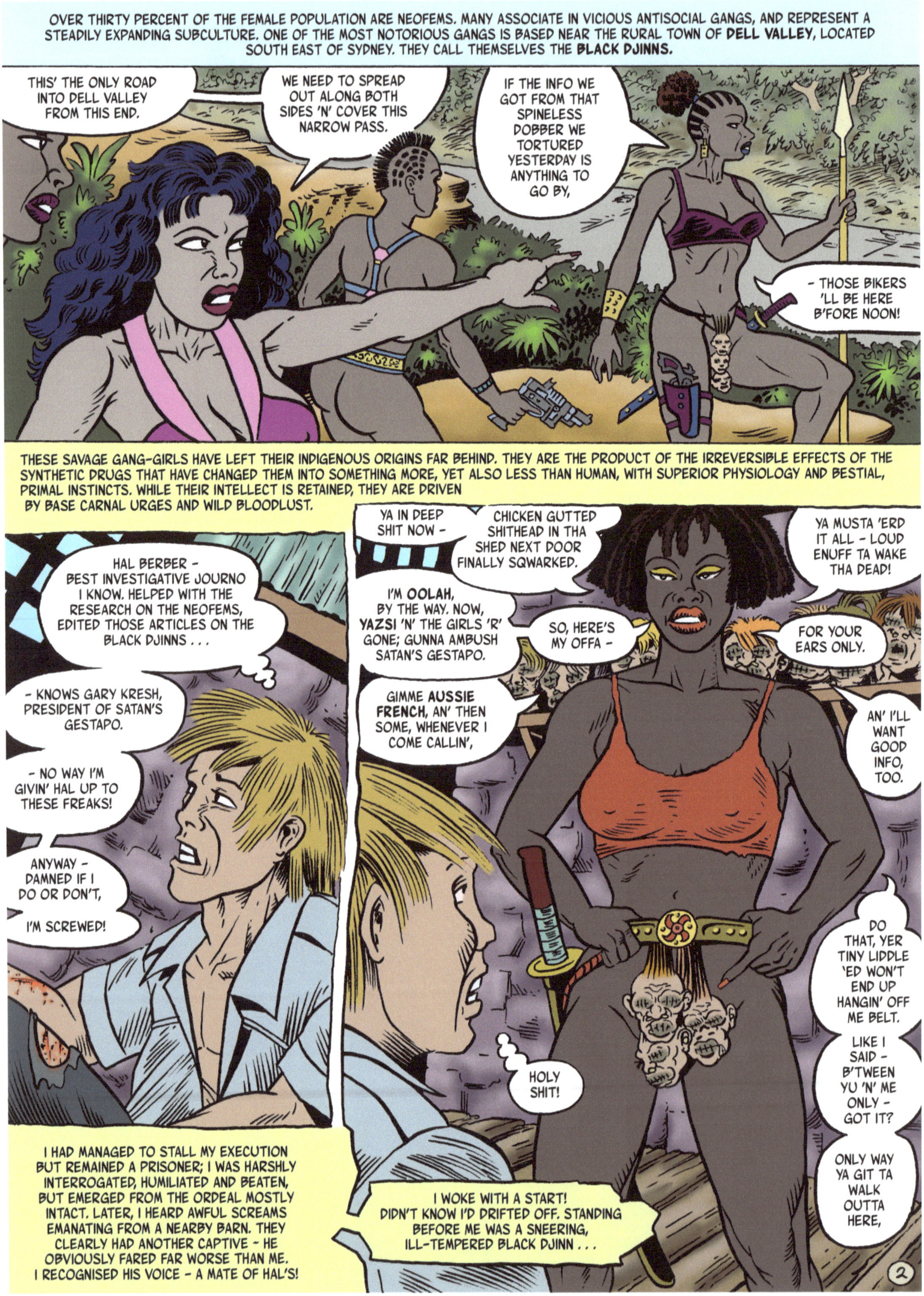

THESE SAVAGE GANG-GIRLS HAVE LEFT THEIR INDIGENOUS ORIGINS FAR BEHIND. THEY ARE THE PRODUCT OF THE IRREVERSIBLE EFFECTS OF THE SYNTHETIC DRUGS THAT HAVE CHANGED THEM INTO SOMETHING MORE, YET ALSO LESS THAN HUMAN, WITH SUPERIOR PHYSIOLOGY AND BESTIAL, PRIMAL INSTINCTS. WHILE THEIR INTELLECT IS RETAINED, THEY ARE DRIVEN BY BASE CARNAL URGES AND WILD BLOODLUST.

I HAD MANAGED TO STALL MY EXECUTION BUT REMAINED A PRISONER; I WAS HARSHLY INTERROGATED, HUMILIATED AND BEATEN, BUT EMERGED FROM THE ORDEAL MOSTLY INTACT. LATER, I HEARD AWFUL SCREAMS EMANATING FROM A NEARBY BARN. THEY CLEARLY HAD ANOTHER CAPTIVE - HE OBVIOUSLY FARED FAR WORSE THAN ME. I RECOGNISED HIS VOICE - A MATE OF HAL'S!

I WOKE WITH A START! DIDN'T KNOW I'D DRIFTED OFF. STANDING BEFORE ME WAS A SNEERING, ILL-TEMPERED BLACK DJINN . . .

ONE MORE THING – YOU'LL BE WRITIN' REAL NICE THINGS 'BOUT US BLACK DJINNS IN THAT DUNNY ROLL YU CALL THA LOCAL PAPER!
SURE – WHATEVER YOU WANT . . .
GIVEN MY SITUATION WHAT ELSE COULD I SAY?
OMINOUS GROWLS AND LOUD SHRIEKS SUDDENLY RENT THE AIR. WHATEVER CAUSED THEM WAS DISTURBINGLY CLOSE . . .
THE IRATE NEOFEM QUICKLY DREW HER SWORD ––
YOU STAY HERE, OR I'LL LOP YA STUPID HEAD CLEAR OFF!
A SECOND LATER SHE WAS GONE. BEING IN SUCH A RUSH SHE'D FORGOTTEN TO LOCK THE DOOR – I WAITED FOR A MINUTE OR SO, THEN CREPT OUTSIDE.
MANDREGS!
THEY WERE ONCE MEN – HOOKED ON RETROX . . .
THE SUBSTANCE GRADUALLY TURNED THEM INTO HIDEOUS, SHAMBLING DEFORMED THINGS –
DROOLING, GROPING, GIBBERING – THERE WERE STORIES OF SCORES OF THEM LURKING OUT IN THE COUNTRYSIDE . . .
MOST OF THE BLACK DJINN GANG HAD GONE TO AMBUSH SATAN'S GESTAPO!
AS FOR ME, IT WAS TIME TO SCARPER –

THE BLACK DJINNS' SETTLEMENT IS LOCATED IN THE BUSHY OUTSKIRTS OF DELL VALLEY. I HEARD THE SKREELING WHINE OF TURBO CYCLES — I HAD REACHED THE ROAD.
READY, STEADY . . .
NOW!
SATAN'S GESTAPO!
THEY'RE COMING —
RELEASE THE BUNYIPS!
I WAS STUNNED. THERE THEY WERE — LIVING LEGENDS!
BUNYIPS — MILITARY EXPERIMENTS THAT HAD ESCAPED; ENGINEERED KILLERS THAT ARE A DIABOLICAL FUSION OF MAN AND BEAST —
— THAT'S THE LATEST, MOST POPULAR CONSPIRACY THEORY.
AND RIDING STRAIGHT INTO THE MASSIVE BRUTES WAS SATAN'S GESTAPO'S ELITIST SQUAD OF ASSASSINS — THE CENTURIONS!
4

THERE WERE THREE OF THE CREATURES.
STARTLED AND WOUNDED BY GUNFIRE TWO OF THEM SCRAMBLED INTO THE BUSH.
THE LAST ONE LAY DYING ON THE ROAD.
THREE OF THE CENTURIONS HAD BEEN TORN TO PIECES . . .
. . . AND THE BATTLE HAD JUST BEGUN.
THE DJINNS 'R' ON BOTH SIDES OF THE ROAD!
– KNEW WE WERE COMIN'!
SOMEBODY BLABBED!
FIRST CAME THE FIREFIGHT. BOTH SIDES KILLED FROM A DISTANCE, BEHIND COVER. BUT THE CRAFTY BLACK DJINNS WERE SLOWLY CLOSING IN . . .

EASY 'N' QUIETLY DOES IT, GIRLS.
GARY KRESH'S HEAD –
IS GUNNA LOOK REAL GOOD,
– WHEN IT'S DANGLIN' FROM ME LAP-LAP!

– VERY SOON, IT WAS UP CLOSE 'N' PERSONAL.

I WATCHED, TRANSFIXED, FROM A HIGH LEDGE - BEST SEAT IN THE HOUSE!
SILLY BUGGERS!
WIFF YA STUPID ROMAN HELMETS!
PHUH!
TIME TO BOLT
LONG WAY BACK TO DELL VALLEY!
LAST TWO MAGS!
THERE WAS NOTHING I COULD DO - THE DJINNS HAD TAKEN MY CELL PHONE SO I HAD NO WAY OF CONTACTING THE LOCAL AUTHORITIES.
BITCHES'LL SLAUGHTER US!
CENTURION
TOO MANY OF 'EM!
CENTURIONS! PULL OUT!
I HEARD THE CAPTAIN'S ORDER TO RETREAT, EVEN FROM WAY UP HERE.
UP ON THAT LEDGE, SERGEANT - SOMEONE WATCHIN'.
NOT ONE OF THE DJINNS! A MAN.
THEN WE GOTTA GET 'IM.
I WANT ANSWERS!
BET 'E'S GOT 'EM!
THAT DAY WILL BE REMEMBERED AS A GRIM DEFEAT OF THE ELITIST CENTURIONS.
ALMOST A THIRD OF THEM HAD BEEN BRUTALLY BUTCHERED
THE BLACK DJINNS BELIEVE THAT FEMJOLT GIVES THEM MYSTICAL POWERS AND TURNS THEM INTO SUPERNATURAL WARRIORS, LIKE THE DJINNS OF ANCIENT LEGEND,
AND LIKE PRIMITIVE WARRIORS OF THE PAST, THESE HEADHUNTERS BELIEVE THAT EVERY TROPHY THEY CLAIM IMBUES THEM WITH MORE
6

MANDREGS, BUNYIPS, MAD BIKER ASSASSINS AND CRAZED NEOFEMS!
WHAT ELSE IS LURKIN' OUT HERE?
I'M UNARMED! AS TO WHY I STALLED TO GAZE UPON THAT MASSACRE?
- SEARCH ME!
I HAVE TO GET OUT OF HERE!
MINUTES LATER . . .
NO, NO! II'D NEVER DO THAT! HAL IS MY FRIEND - I HATE THOSE DJINNS AS MUCH AS YOU DO!
YOU! IAN STANLEY - SO YOU'RE THE SNITCH! BETRAYED US, AND YOUR PAL, HAL BERBER, TO THE MAD DJINNS!
I'M GUNNA SHOVE THIS GLADIUS UP YER ARSE - DISEMBOWEL YA!
STOP! YOU GOTTA LISTEN TO ME!
IT'S THE DEATH OF A TRAITOR FOR YOU, WORM!
ALRITE! LET'S HEAR IT - YOU GOT ONE MINUTE, NEWSBOY!
THE DJINNS GOT ME AN' ANOTHER GUY - DIDN'T SEE 'IM BUT I HEARD IT ALL. THINK IT WAS MORT CARSON,
- RECOGNISED THE VOICE.
HE COPPED IT FIRST, THEY TORTURED THE SHIT OUT OF HIM! HE MUST HAVE TOLD 'EM!
DON'T BLAME 'IM. FEW MEN CAN WITHSTAND THEIR TACTICS --
DON'T KNOW THAT I'D HAVE BEEN ABLE TO HOLD OUT ANY LONGER THAN HE DID - BUT IT DIDN'T GET THAT FAR;
MANDREGS ATTACKED THE DJINN'S BASE, I ESCAPED.
THE TRUTH IS - I TOLD THOSE DJINNS NOTHING -
NONE OF US SAW HER -
WHAT DO YOU MAKE OF THAT STORY, CENTURION?
IT'S ALL BULLSHIT, BROTHER.
- DESPERATE TA SAVE 'IS 'IDE. 'E'S A NEWS 'OUND,
KNOWS HOW TA SPIN ONE, AN' A GOOD ONE AT THAT.
YEAH - YOU GOT A GOOD POINT THERE!
7

IT WAS OOLAH – SHE DISPATCHED BOTH OF THEM WITHIN SECONDS ...
THEIR CHAIN-MAIL VESTS MAY JUST AS WELL HAVE BEEN MADE OF PAPER,
YU IN STRIFE BOY! I TOL' YU TA STAY PUT!
... I SAW IT –– A MONSTROSITY STALKING US – LEERING AT ME,
BEHIND YOU – LOOK OUT!
JUS' HOW STUPE DO YU THINK I AM, BOY?
YA GUNNA HAFTA DO BEDDA 'N THAT!
SHE WAS SO CONVINCED IT WAS A RUSE SHE DIDN'T BOTHER TO LOOK.
SKST!
THE SUBHUMAN CREATURE POUNCED.
I KNEW IT WANTED ME,
– BUT OOLAH PRESENTED AN OBSTACLE AND A THREAT ...
8

WHEN A WOMAN BECOMES A NEOFEM SHE IS NO LONGER DEPENDENT ON FEMJOLT OR RETROX. THE SAME APPLIES FOR MEN WHO HAVE BEEN TRANSFORMED BY THESE DRUGS.
THIS FACT DOES NOT STOP PEOPLE FROM USING THEM; THE SIDE EFFECTS ARE OFTEN DEVASTATING, ESPECIALLY FROM RETROX. SEVERE RETROGRESSIVE MUTATION OCCURS; NEOFEMS ARE TRANSFORMED INTO HORRIFYING CREATURES CALLED RETROFEMS.
MY FATE RESTED ON WHAT ACTION I NOW CHOSE . . .
OOLAH HAD LOST HER WEAPON. HER INHUMAN ATTACKER GAINED THE ADVANTAGE --
IF THE RETROFEM PREVAILED I STOOD NO CHANCE; THERE WERE ONLY SECONDS TO SPARE . . . I PICKED UP OOLAH'S WEAPON,
HAD SHE NOT TURNED UP AND SLAIN THOSE TWO CENTURIONS I'D BE DEAD.
THAT THOUGHT BURNED IN MY MIND AS I STRUCK THE CRAZED RETROFEM.
SAVING OOLAH FROM CERTAIN DEATH DID NOT ENSURE THAT SHE WOULD SPARE MY LIFE IN RETURN.
THE BLACK DJINNS LIVE BY A CODE OF SAVAGE RETRIBUTION AND BRUTAL VIOLENCE. REGARDLESS, I FELT COMPELLED TO ACT . . .
ONCE AGAIN - DAMNED IF I DO, DAMNED IF I DON'T! 9

ALRITE, I OWE YA ONE - YA GET TA KEEP YA HEAD, THA DEAL B'TWEEN YU AN' ME STILL STANDS -
- AN' THAT MEANS JUS' YU' AN' ME, GOT IT!
YU NEED TA KNOW - WE'RE THA ONLY THING STANDIN' B'TWEEN DELL VALLEY AN' A HOSTILE TAKEOVER BY SATAN'S GESTAPO. IF YU FIND OUT SOM'FIN I SHOULD KNOW, YU BEDDA TELL ME!
ALRITE, YOU CUN GO!
- HAL BERBER FLED TOWN, A FUGITIVE OF THE BLACK DJINNS; GARY KRESH'S HEAD DIDN'T WIND UP DANGLING FROM YAZSI'S WAIST.
DAY'S AFTER FLEEING THE BATTLE BETWEEN THE CENTURIONS AND THE BLACK DJINN GANG GIRLS HE WAS KILLED DURING A RECON MISSION BY ONE OF THE MARAUDING BUNYIPS.
YOU CAN READ ALL ABOUT IT IN A SPECIAL EDITION OF THAT "DUNNY ROLL" OOLAH CALLS THE LOCAL PAPER. IT IS DUE FOR RELEASE VERY SOON.
OF COURSE, CERTAIN FACTS WILL BE OMITTED TO PROTECT THE GUILTY, AND THE INTEGRITY OF THE "SPECIAL RELATIONS" BETWEEN OOLAH AND ME.
FIN

EASY PREY
WITHIN THE RUIN, THERE WAS FOOD. THIS, JESRIC KNEW FOR CERTAIN, NOW. EVEN THOUGH ON FIRST IMPRESSION, THE RUIN SEEMED AS UNINHABITED AS ANY OTHER . . .
THREE DAYS AGO, THE RODENT HAD RUN INTO A MOUND OF RUBBLE STREWN AROUND A LONG FORGOTTEN BUILDING. WHILE RUMMAGING THROUGH THE REFUSE, JESRIC FOUND PROOF OF LIFE WITHIN.
THE PLACE REEKED OF MAN SCENT. THAT'S RIGHT - MAN SCENT.
MAN - WHO LEFT THE WORLD IN CHAOS. MAN - WHO ERADICATED HIS ENVIRONMENT AND HIMSELF WITH IT.
MAN - A FRAIL, WEAK BEING WHO HAD NO PLACE ON THIS NEW EARTH. THOSE HE LEFT BEHIND FINALLY SLUNK OUT OF THE SHADOWS - AFTER AEONS OF HIDING - TO INHERIT A WASTELAND.
FRANKIE LANE
COKE
STORY & SCRIPT BY STEVE CARTER © 1987
SCRIPT REVISED 2016 BY STEVE CARTER & ANTOINETTE RYDYR
ART - DILLON - © 1987

JESRIC CIRCLED THE LURCHING STRUCTURE SEVERAL TIMES BUT THERE WAS NO WAY UP TO WHERE THE MAN LIVED. HE CRAWLED BENEATH IT, BETWEEN MOULDY PYLONS AND BEAMS, OVER MORE RUBBLE. THERE, JESRIC HEARD THE MECHANICAL AND ELECTRIC HUMMING OF MAN'S MACHINES SOFTLY EBBING INTO THE NIGHT.
FROM AN OBSCURE APERTURE ABOVE, A WAN BEAM OF LIGHT BATHED THE DEVASTATION BELOW, CASTING WEIRD SHADOWS. IT REVEALED THE MEANS TO ENTER THE PART OF THE ABODE WHERE THE MAN WORKED AND LIVED.
THE APERTURE WAS TOO HIGH TO REACH AND DESPITE ALL THE DEBRIS LYING AROUND, JESRIC COULD FIND NOTHING TO SPAN THE GAP.
THE MAN NEEDED LIGHT TO WORK HIS MACHINES. JESRIC KNEW THE LIGHT WAS ARTIFICIAL. UNLIKE JESRIC AND HIS KIN, MAN WAS UNABLE TO SEE IN THE DARK WITHOUT AID.
HE REMEMBERED SEEING AN OBJECT HE COULD USE. THE NEXT DAY HE SET ON A FIVE MILE JOURNEY TO OBTAIN IT.

JESRIC'S DESTINATION WAS THE *VALLEY OF ZOMBIES*. LYING SCATTERED IN THE DISORDER OF POST DESTRUCTION WERE COUNTLESS LENGTHS OF SCAFFOLDING, MOST OF THEM TWISTED, MELTED. AFTER HALF A DAY OF SEARCHING WHILE AVOIDING OR FENDING OFF THE MEANDERING AND LUMBERING *LIVING DEAD*, JESRIC FOUND A RELATIVELY STRAIGHT AND LENGTHY GIRDER.

THE DWELLING WAS AN IMMENSE *VAULT*. ALL WINDOWS WERE SEALED, SHUTTING OUT NATURAL LIGHT. MOST OF THE FLOORSPACE WAS TAKEN UP BY *BULKY MACHINERY*, THE PURPOSE OF WHICH WAS *UNKNOWN* TO THE INTRUDER.

JESRIC CLIMBED UP THE MACHINERY AND *STEALTHILY* CRAWLED ALONG THE TOP, LEAPING FROM ONE MACHINE BULK TO THE NEXT.

UPON HIS RETURN TO THE RUIN, IT WAS *DARK* AND *SILENT*. THE MACHINES HAD STOPPED WHIRRING. CAREFULLY, JESRIC POSITIONED THE BEAM.

HE JAMMED ONE END INTO THE CHASSIS OF A DECAYED AUTOMOBILE AND RESTED THE OTHER END AGAINST THE APERTURE'S EDGE. THE GIRDER CREAKED AND BOWED UNDER HIS WEIGHT. JESRIC SCALED THE STEEP INCLINE – BRIDGING *MAN'S DOMAIN* AND HIS *OWN WORLD*.

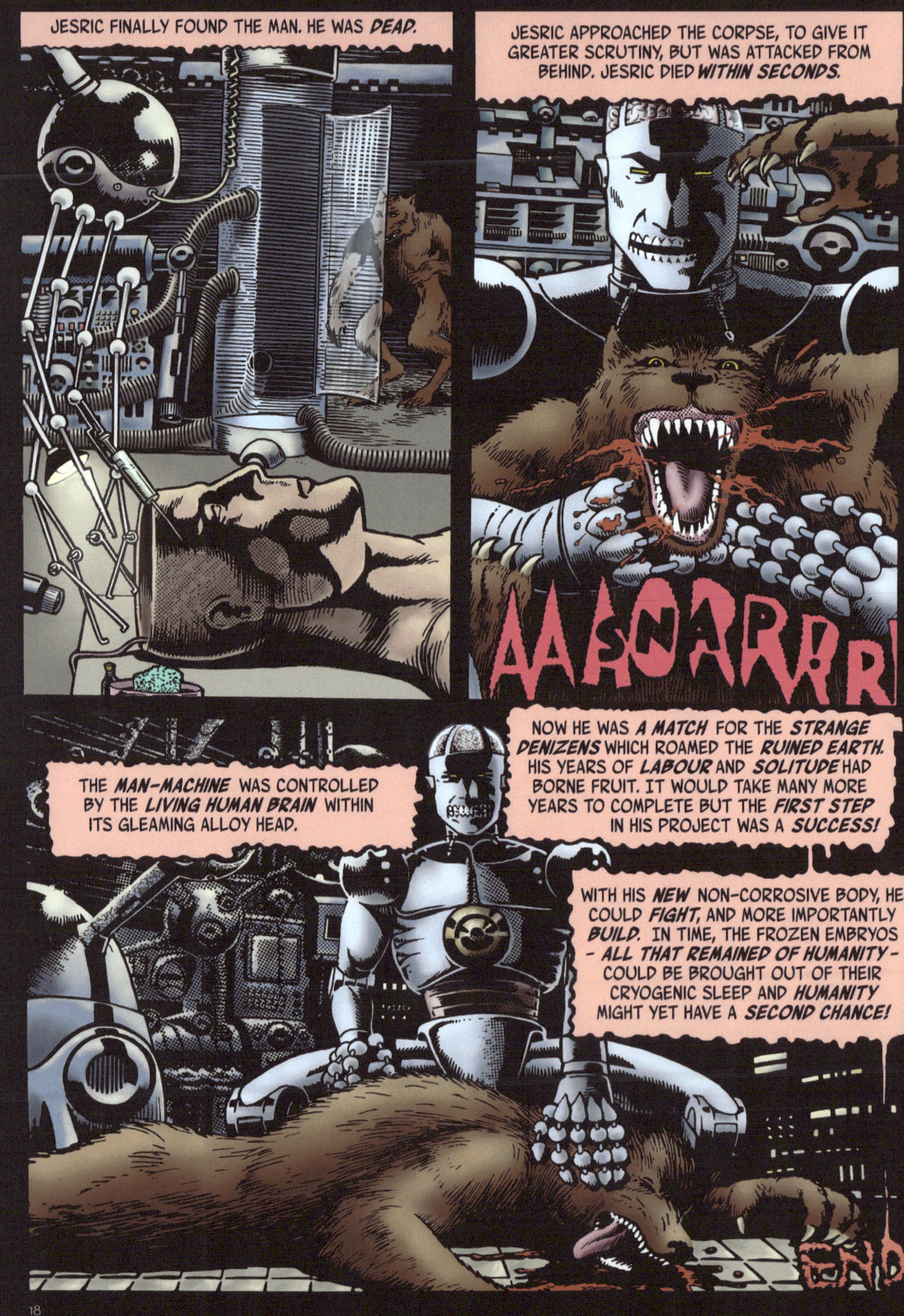
JESRIC FINALLY FOUND THE MAN. HE WAS DEAD.
JESRIC APPROACHED THE CORPSE, TO GIVE IT GREATER SCRUTINY, BUT WAS ATTACKED FROM BEHIND. JESRIC DIED WITHIN SECONDS.
AASNARRR
THE MAN-MACHINE WAS CONTROLLED BY THE LIVING HUMAN BRAIN WITHIN ITS GLEAMING ALLOY HEAD.
NOW HE WAS A MATCH FOR THE STRANGE DENIZENS WHICH ROAMED THE RUINED EARTH. HIS YEARS OF LABOUR AND SOLITUDE HAD BORNE FRUIT. IT WOULD TAKE MANY MORE YEARS TO COMPLETE BUT THE FIRST STEP IN HIS PROJECT WAS A SUCCESS!
WITH HIS NEW NON-CORROSIVE BODY, HE COULD FIGHT, AND MORE IMPORTANTLY BUILD. IN TIME, THE FROZEN EMBRYOS - ALL THAT REMAINED OF HUMANITY - COULD BE BROUGHT OUT OF THEIR CRYOGENIC SLEEP AND HUMANITY MIGHT YET HAVE A SECOND CHANCE!
END

REAP WHAT YOU SOW
BY STEVE CARTER AND ANTOINETTE RYDYR © 2009
THIS IS A TERRIBLE DAY, BROTHER PETERSON!
IT MIGHT BE THE END OF THE WORLD AS WE KNOW IT!
YES, FATHER.
I'M TOLD THEY ARE CALLED THE VULCANIAN VALKYRIE!
POWERFUL DENIZENS OF THE DESERT OF BURNING SIN HAVE MANIFESTED UPON OUR HOLY FATHER'S BLESSED EARTH!
EVIDENTLY, THEY ARE THE EMBODIMENT OF THE BITTER SPIRITS OF EVERY WOMAN THAT EVER SUFFERED UNDER THE YOKE OF RELIGIOUS PERSECUTIONS.
AND UNLIKE OTHER DWELLERS OF THAT GOD-FORSAKEN REALM, SLAYING THEM WILL NOT SEND THEM BACK THERE. THEY BURN, THEN RISE AGAIN FROM THEIR SMOULDERING ASKES LIKE MALEVOLENT PHOENIX!

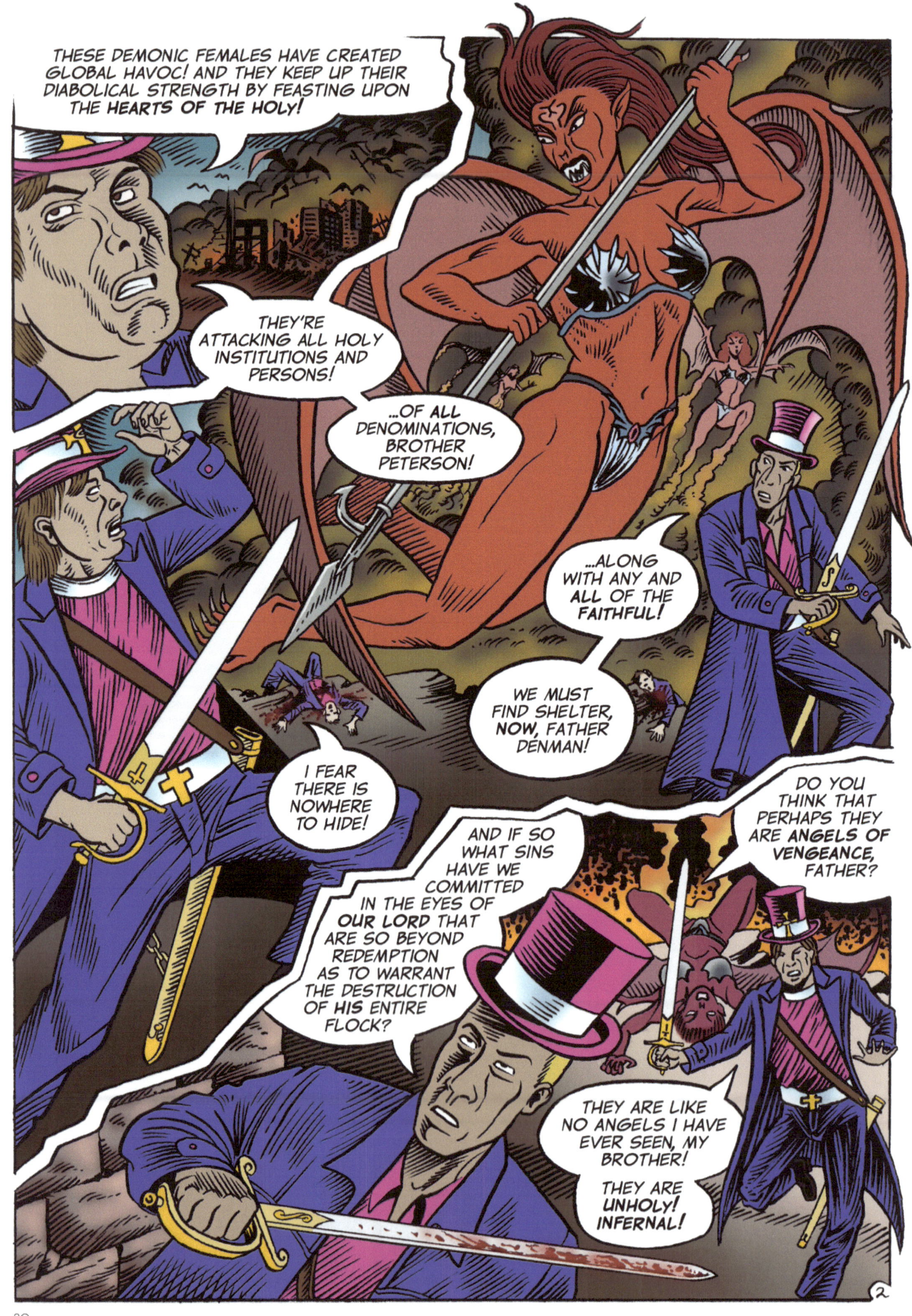

THESE DEMONIC FEMALES HAVE CREATED GLOBAL HAVOC! AND THEY KEEP UP THEIR DIABOLICAL STRENGTH BY FEASTING UPON THE HEARTS OF THE HOLY!
THEY'RE ATTACKING ALL HOLY INSTITUTIONS AND PERSONS!
...OF ALL DENOMINATIONS, BROTHER PETERSON!
...ALONG WITH ANY AND ALL OF THE FAITHFUL!
WE MUST FIND SHELTER, NOW, FATHER DENMAN!
I FEAR THERE IS NOWHERE TO HIDE!
AND IF SO WHAT SINS HAVE WE COMMITTED IN THE EYES OF OUR LORD THAT ARE SO BEYOND REDEMPTION AS TO WARRANT THE DESTRUCTION OF HIS ENTIRE FLOCK?
DO YOU THINK THAT PERHAPS THEY ARE ANGELS OF VENGEANCE, FATHER?
THEY ARE LIKE NO ANGELS I HAVE EVER SEEN, MY BROTHER!
THEY ARE UNHOLY! INFERNAL!

...THE HOUSE OF OUR LORD AND SAVIOUR ...IN RUINS.
FATHER DENMAN!
HORRIBLE MOMENTS LATER,
HUMANITY CAN BE DIVIDED INTO TWO DISTINCT GROUPS,
THOSE WHO ARE RELIGIOUS AND THOSE WHO ARE NOT!
AND IT IS RELIGION THAT REPRESENTS THE GREATER EVIL!

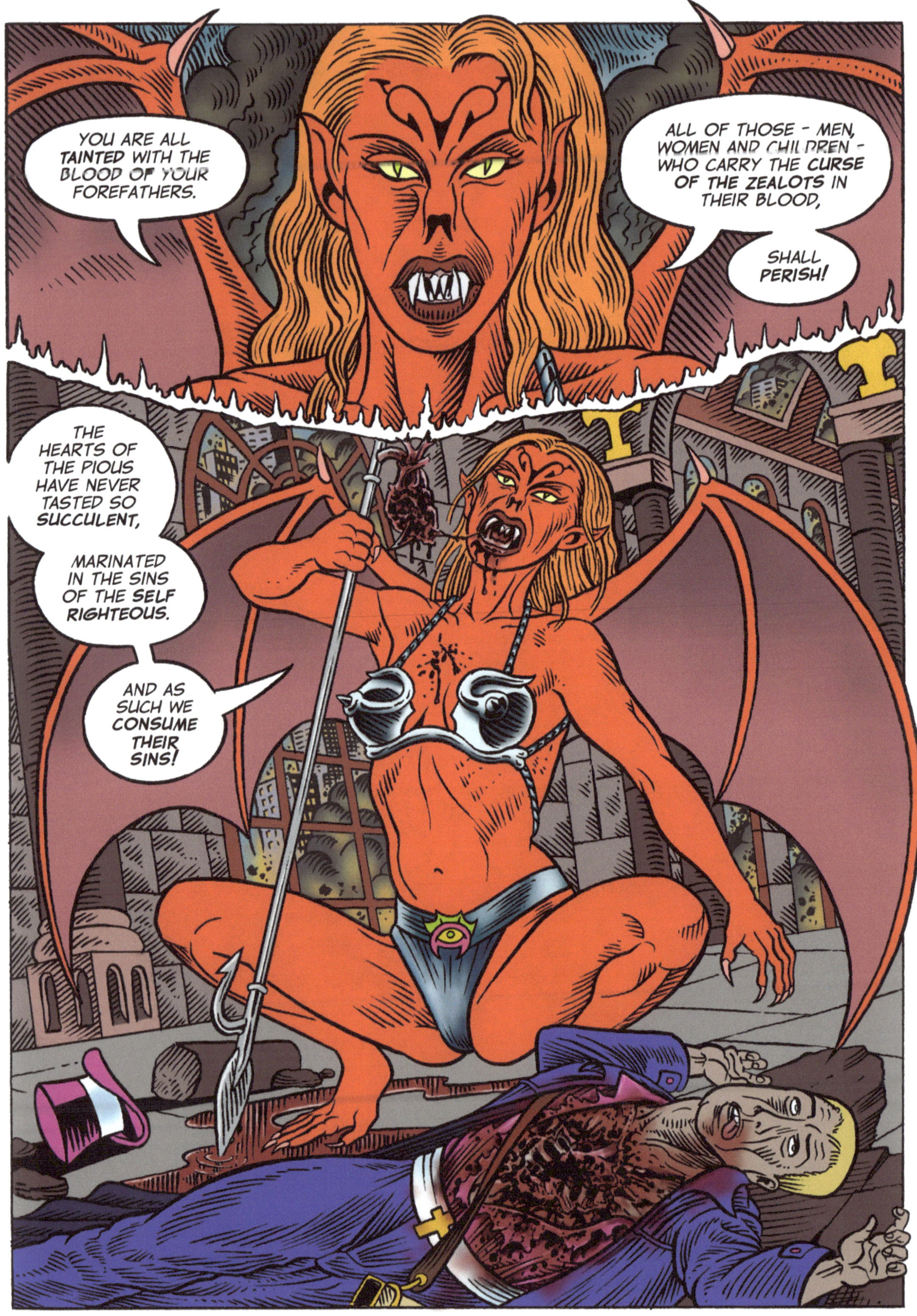

YOU ARE ALL TAINTED WITH THE BLOOD OF YOUR FOREFATHERS.
ALL OF THOSE - MEN, WOMEN AND CHILDREN - WHO CARRY THE CURSE OF THE ZEALOTS IN THEIR BLOOD,
SHALL PERISH!
THE HEARTS OF THE PIOUS HAVE NEVER TASTED SO SUCCULENT,
MARINATED IN THE SINS OF THE SELF RIGHTEOUS.
AND AS SUCH WE CONSUME THEIR SINS!

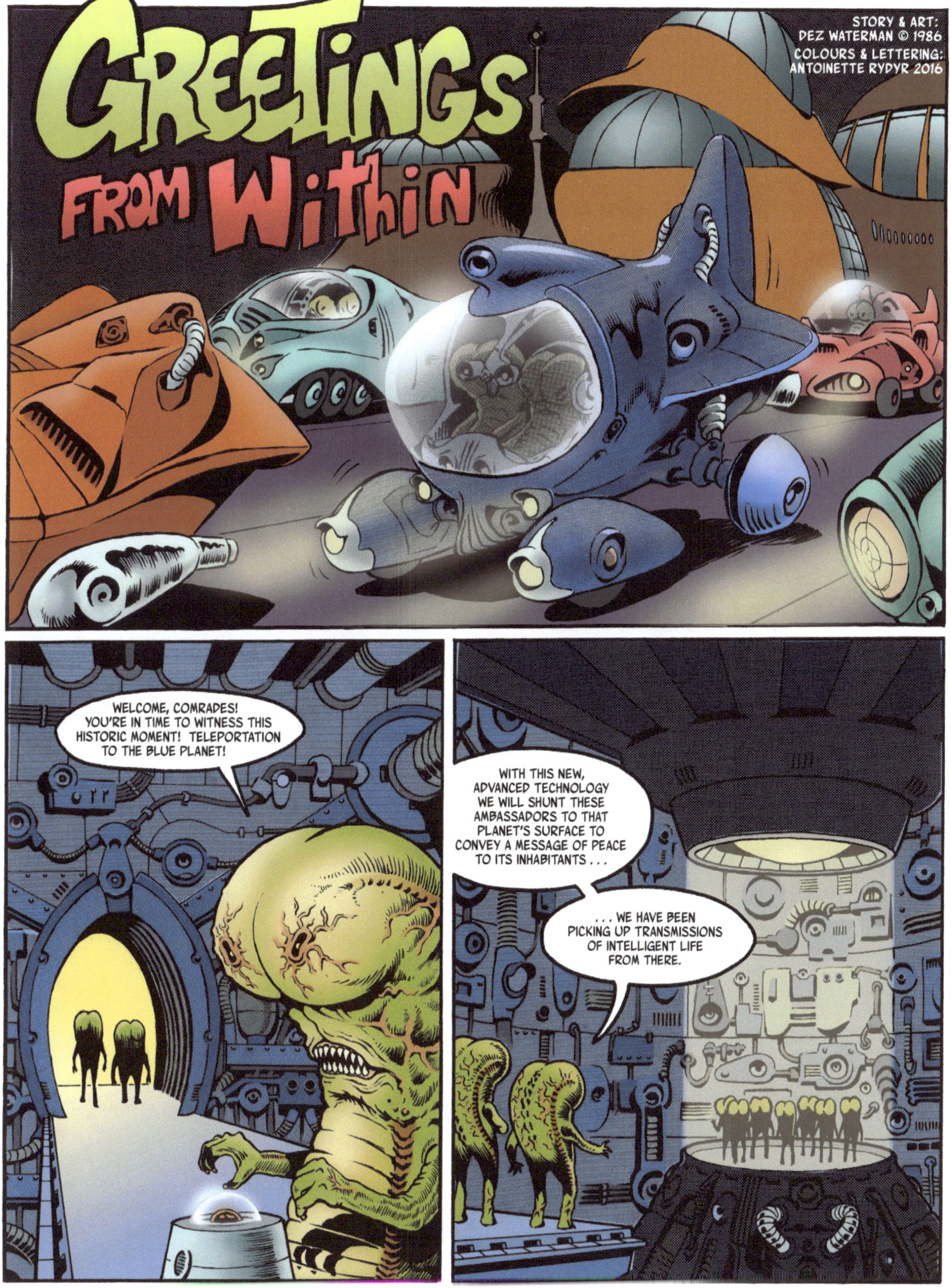

Greetings From Within

THE LONG RANGE SCANNER WILL ALLOW US TO KEEP IN CONSTANT COMMUNICATION.
AND NOW . . . LET THE JOURNEY COMMENCE.
A GIANT ENERGY FIELD SURGED INTO ACTION. THE SEVEN *TRINEON* AMBASSADORS WERE CONVERTED INTO PURE MOLECULAR PLASMA AND BEAMED INTO SPACE . . .

. . . WHERE THEY TRAVERSED COUNTLESS LIGHT YEARS IN MERE HOURS . . .

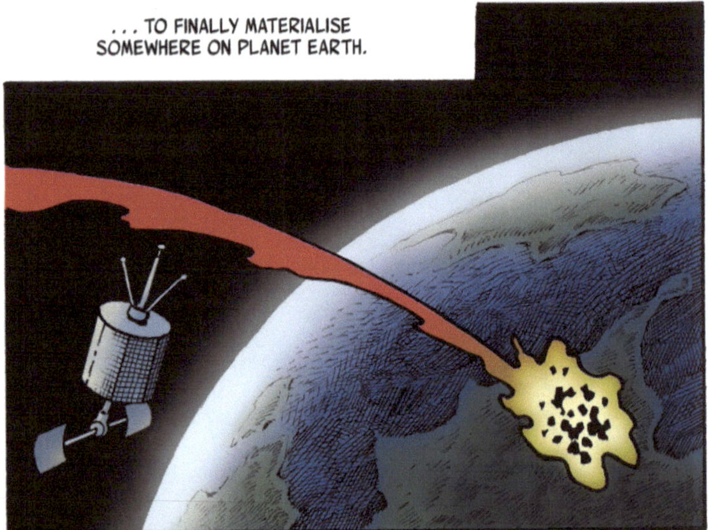

. . . TO FINALLY MATERIALISE SOMEWHERE ON PLANET EARTH.

MEANWHILE . . .
GOD DAMNED STOMACH! PAIN'S GETTING WORSE ALL THE TIME!
NO SMOKING!
CHILD ABU
IT'S EVERY ONE'S BUSI
IF YOU KNOW OR SUSPECT AN
EVEN FRIENDS OR FAMILY M
DON'T HESITAT   CONTA
DOB
-LINE
CANCER
ANCES ARE YOU'VE
T AND DON'T KNOW!
BRAIN CANCER

MR JOHNSTONE, THE DOCTOR WILL SEE YOU NOW.

HI, DOC!
HELLO, MR JOHNSTONE. AND WHAT CAN I DO FOR YOU?

WELL DOC, IT'S THESE STOMACH PAINS I'VE BEEN HAVING. I'VE NO IDEA WHAT'S CAUSING THEM.
WELL, IT'S MY JOB TO FIND OUT. PERHAPS YOU COULD DESCRIBE THE PAINS FOR ME.
SURE.

I'LL JUST REMOVE MY JACKET . . .
LET'S SEE, IT'S SORT OF LIKE A DULL ACHE . . .

IT THROBS A BIT, TOO. IT SORT OF STARTS OVER HERE . . . KIND OF MOVES SLOWLY OVER HERE AND THEN . . .
OUCH!
MY GOD!
NOW THAT HURT!

CAN YOU DESCRIBE IT?
THIS ONES DIFFERENT, DOC! THIS IS . . .
OOOCH!
TELL ME!
IT'S, IT'S . . .
MY GOD!

WHAT'S HAPPENING?!
OOO-AAH!!
. . . IT'S MOVING!
UH-OUCH!
IT'S MOVING! GOD, IT'S MOVING!

AAAHHH!!
TEARING UP MY INSIDES . . . TRYING TO GET OUT!
OUCH!
THE PAIN!
HELP ME!!

AAAARRGH!

GLURK GLOG...

YOU GUYS ALRIGHT?
WHAT A PLACE TO COME DOWN!
ALMOST ASPHIXIATED IN THERE!
BEAM US BACK PROMPTLY! WE'VE MADE A TERRIBLE ERROR!

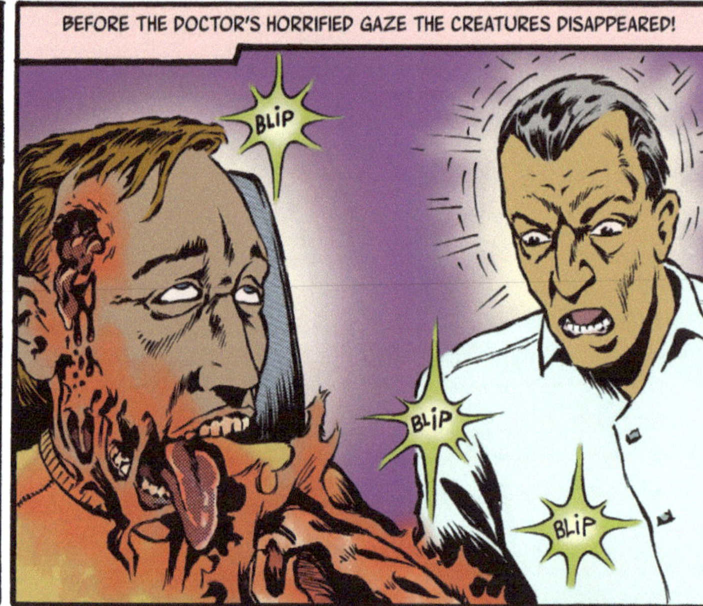

BEFORE THE DOCTOR'S HORRIFIED GAZE THE CREATURES DISAPPEARED!
BLIP
BLIP
BLIP

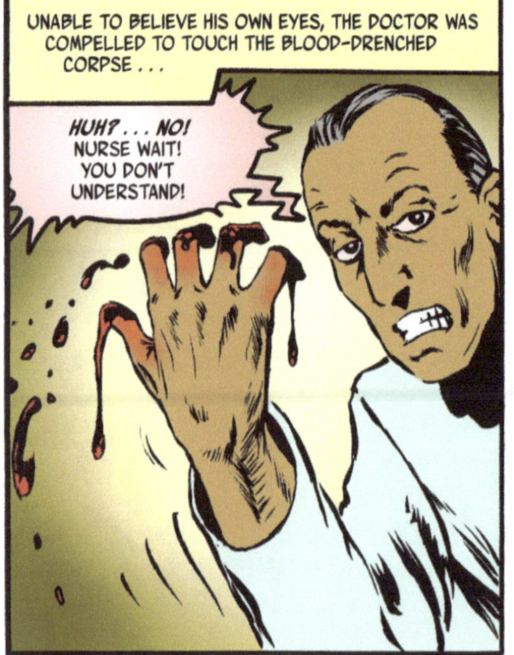

UNABLE TO BELIEVE HIS OWN EYES, THE DOCTOR WAS COMPELLED TO TOUCH THE BLOOD-DRENCHED CORPSE...
HUH?... NO! NURSE WAIT! YOU DON'T UNDERSTAND!

THE LITTLE GREEN MEN! IT WAS THE LITTLE GREEN MEN...
SURE IT WAS, DOCTOR... SURE IT WAS.
END

BY *STEVE CARTER* & *ANTOINETTE RYDYR* © 2010 BASED ON *WAR OF THE AMAZULU AND AMAZOMBI* © 2009 S.C.A.R.

PLANET NEMESIS — THE VALLEY OF **M'B LANURIS** IN THE SOUTHEASTERN FRINGES OF THE **DRETHERIAN JUNGLE**, DOMAIN OF THE **UBARI**.

THE UBARI ARE THE MOST DOMINANT OF A DIVERSE GROUP OF TRIBAL AMAZONS INHABITING THE REGION THAT SHARE A COMMON ANCESTRY.

THE WOMEN ARE POWERFULLY MUSCLED. TERRANS CALL THESE AMAZONS **SLAMAZONS** BECAUSE THEIR PHYSIQUE RESEMBLES THAT OF THE POPULAR TERRAN GLADIATORAL SPORTS TEAM, GROGAN'S SLAMMERS.

COLOURS BY *ANTOINETTE RYDYR* & *STEVE CARTER* © 2012

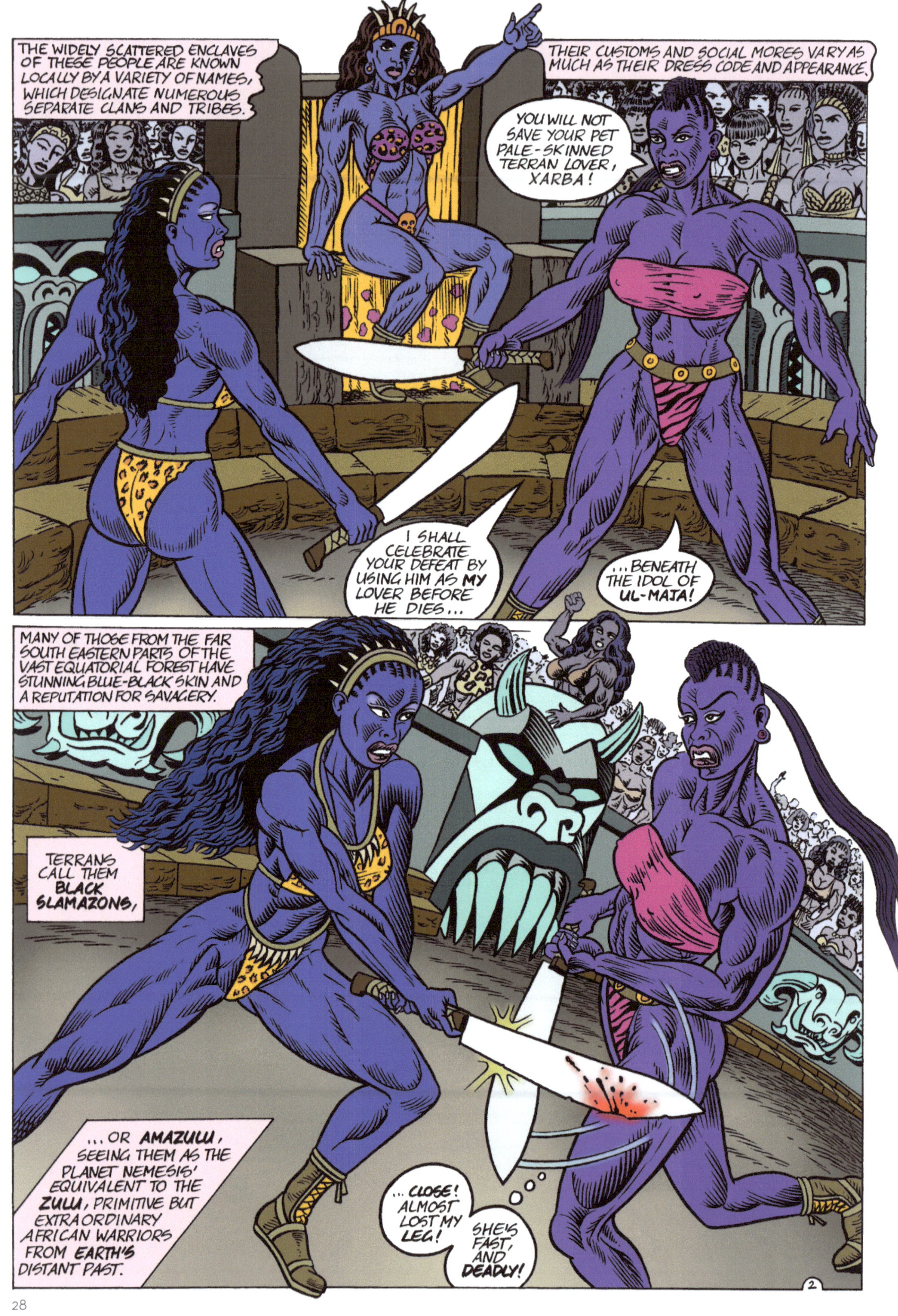

THE WIDELY SCATTERED ENCLAVES OF THESE PEOPLE ARE KNOWN LOCALLY BY A VARIETY OF NAMES, WHICH DESIGNATE NUMEROUS SEPARATE CLANS AND TRIBES.
THEIR CUSTOMS AND SOCIAL MORES VARY AS MUCH AS THEIR DRESS CODE AND APPEARANCE.
YOU WILL NOT SAVE YOUR PET PALE-SKINNED TERRAN LOVER, XARBA!
I SHALL CELEBRATE YOUR DEFEAT BY USING HIM AS MY LOVER BEFORE HE DIES...
...BENEATH THE IDOL OF UL-MAJA!
MANY OF THOSE FROM THE FAR SOUTH EASTERN PARTS OF THE VAST EQUATORIAL FOREST HAVE STUNNING BLUE-BLACK SKIN AND A REPUTATION FOR SAVAGERY.
TERRANS CALL THEM BLACK SLAMAZONS,
...OR AMAZULU, SEEING THEM AS THE PLANET NEMESIS' EQUIVALENT TO THE ZULU, PRIMITIVE BUT EXTRAORDINARY AFRICAN WARRIORS FROM EARTH'S DISTANT PAST.
...CLOSE! ALMOST LOST MY LEG!
SHE'S FAST, AND DEADLY!

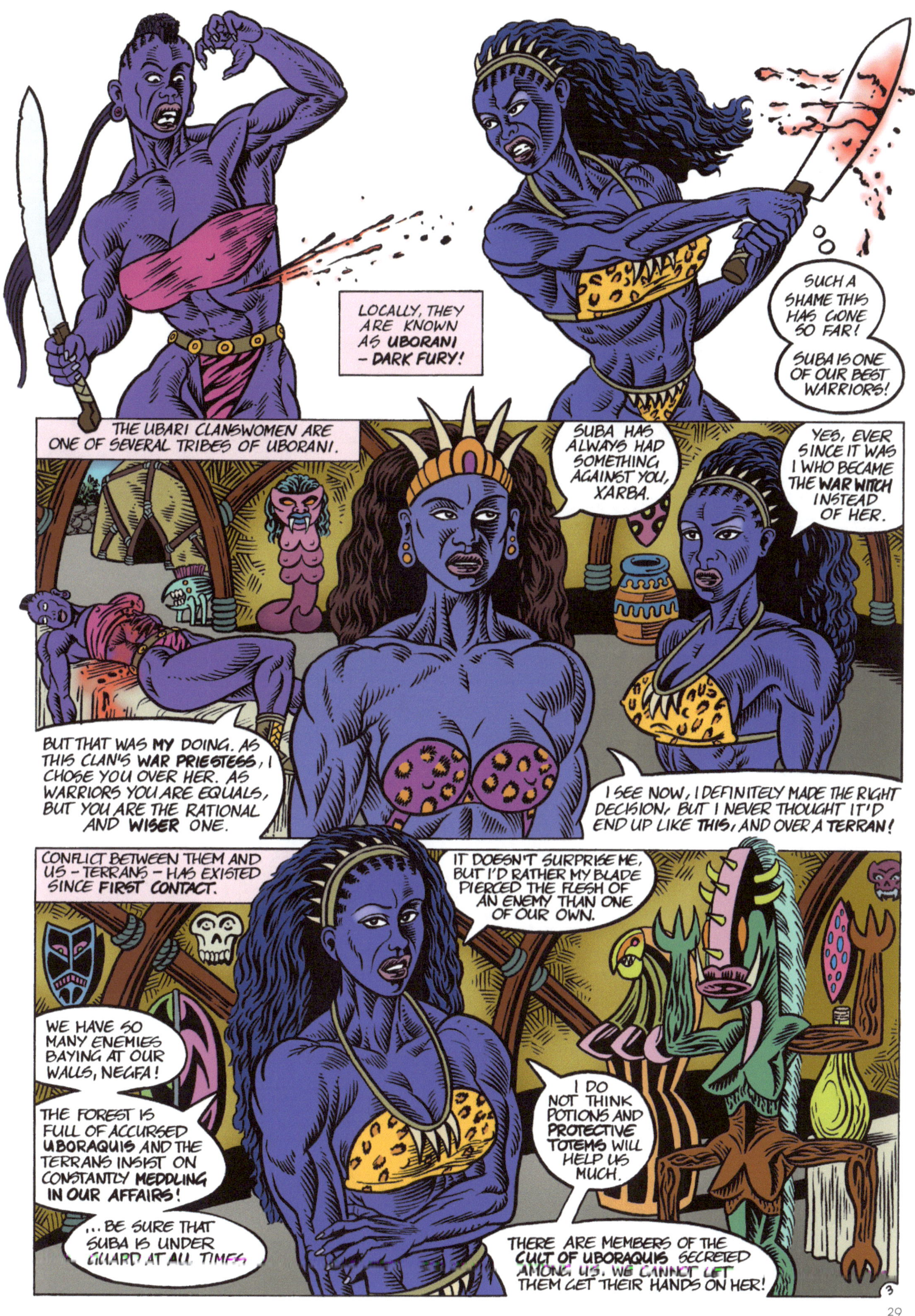

LOCALLY, THEY ARE KNOWN AS UBORANI — DARK FURY!
SUCH A SHAME THIS HAS GONE SO FAR! SUBA IS ONE OF OUR BEST WARRIORS!
THE UBARI CLANSWOMEN ARE ONE OF SEVERAL TRIBES OF UBORANI.
SUBA HAS ALWAYS HAD SOMETHING AGAINST YOU, XARBA.
YES, EVER SINCE IT WAS I WHO BECAME THE WAR WITCH INSTEAD OF HER.
BUT THAT WAS MY DOING. AS THIS CLAN'S WAR PRIESTESS, I CHOSE YOU OVER HER. AS WARRIORS YOU ARE EQUALS, BUT YOU ARE THE RATIONAL AND WISER ONE.
I SEE NOW, I DEFINITELY MADE THE RIGHT DECISION, BUT I NEVER THOUGHT IT'D END UP LIKE THIS, AND OVER A TERRAN!
CONFLICT BETWEEN THEM AND US - TERRANS - HAS EXISTED SINCE FIRST CONTACT.
IT DOESN'T SURPRISE ME, BUT I'D RATHER MY BLADE PIERCED THE FLESH OF AN ENEMY THAN ONE OF OUR OWN.
WE HAVE SO MANY ENEMIES BAYING AT OUR WALLS, NEGFA!
THE FOREST IS FULL OF ACCURSED UBORAQUIS AND THE TERRANS INSIST ON CONSTANTLY MEDDLING IN OUR AFFAIRS!
...BE SURE THAT SUBA IS UNDER GUARD AT ALL TIMES.
I DO NOT THINK POTIONS AND PROTECTIVE TOTEMS WILL HELP US MUCH.
THERE ARE MEMBERS OF THE CULT OF UBORAQUIS SECRETED AMONG US. WE CANNOT LET THEM GET THEIR HANDS ON HER!

ZRAT!
HUMAN BONES! GHASTLY PILES OF THEM INSIDE THAT ANCIENT TEMPLE!
THAT HIDEOUS IDOL, AND THESE UBORANI – BLACK SLAMAZONS, AMAZULU!
...GOT TO BE A CONNECTION!
IN MY DESPERATION TO ESCAPE A FIERCE BAND OF UBORANI I BECAME LOST IN THE FORBIDDING VALLEY OF M'B LANURIS.

AND IF THEY GET ME I'LL WIND UP AMONG THOSE BONES OF THE DEAD.

UBORAQUIS! I HAD RUN STRAIGHT INTO THEM! UP UNTIL THAT MOMENT I HAD BEEN SKEPTICAL OF THE EXISTENCE OF THESE CREATURES!

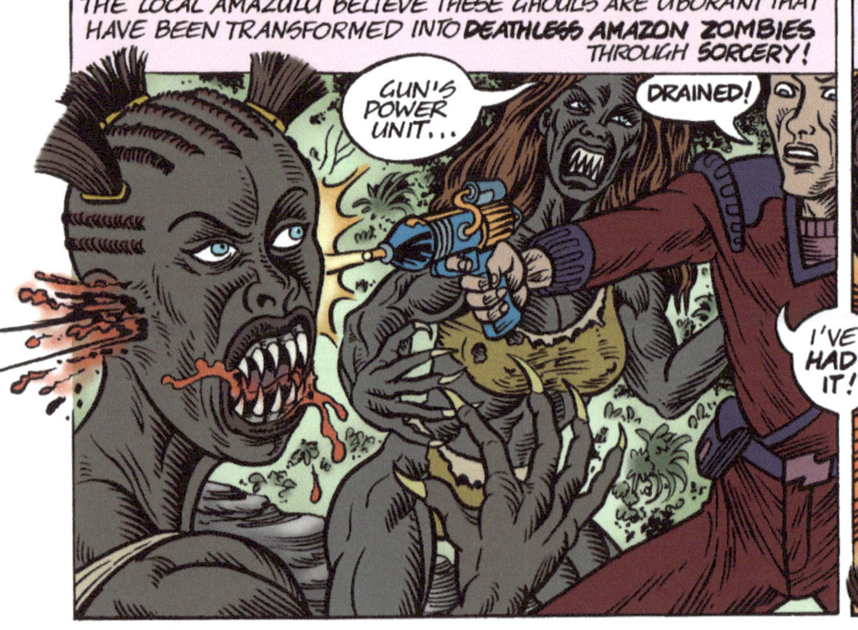

THE LOCAL AMAZULU BELIEVE THESE GHOULS ARE UBORANI THAT HAVE BEEN TRANSFORMED INTO DEATHLESS AMAZON ZOMBIES THROUGH SORCERY!
GUN'S POWER UNIT...
DRAINED!

COLLEAGUES FROM THE TERRAN BASE WHERE I HAD BEEN STATIONED REFERRED TO THESE MYTHOLOGICAL MONSTERS AS AMAZOMBIES!
K'NELL!
WHA...?!
I'VE HAD IT!

A FEW OF THEM CLAIMED THEY HAD SEEN SUCH CREATURES WHEN CONDUCTING EXCAVATIONS AMID THE SCATTERED RUINS WITHIN THIS MYSTERIOUS VALLEY...
A TERRAN, IN OUR TERRITORY!
HE'S OURS!
— CLAIMS I HAD DISMISSED!

I HAD INADVERTENTLY STUMBLED INTO THE REALM OF THE UBARI. RELATIONS BETWEEN THEM AND TERRANS HAD ALL BUT DETERIORATED.
N'GARI, NOW THAT THEY'RE FINALLY CUT TO PIECES, BURN THOSE DEMON UB ORAQUIS. BE SURE THEY CANNOT BE RESURRECTED!
AS FOR THE TERRAN, BRING HIM!
...THOSE AMAZOMBIES! THAT LEWD, WANTON LOOK IN THEIR EYES! EATING FLESH WASN'T ALL THEY CRAVED!

LIKE MANY UBARI, XARBA SPOKE FLUENT TERRAN.
WHY HAVE YOU COME HERE, SPYING AND SCHEMING? EVEN YOUR OWN PEOPLE FORBID YOU TO COME INTO OUR DOMAIN.
WE HAVE DISCOVERED AND EXCAVATED A VASTLY ANCIENT CITY AND I BELIEVE WHAT WE HAVE LEARNED ABOUT IT WILL BE OF GREAT INTEREST TO YOUR PEOPLE.
AS I'VE EXPLAINED, I'M AN ARCHAEOLOGIST AND ANTHROPOLOGIST. I STUDY THE ANCIENT RUINS, OLD RELICS AND THE CUSTOMS OF DIFFERENT PEOPLES.
I AM NOT A WARRIOR OR SOLDIER, OR YOUR ENEMY.
HOW SO?

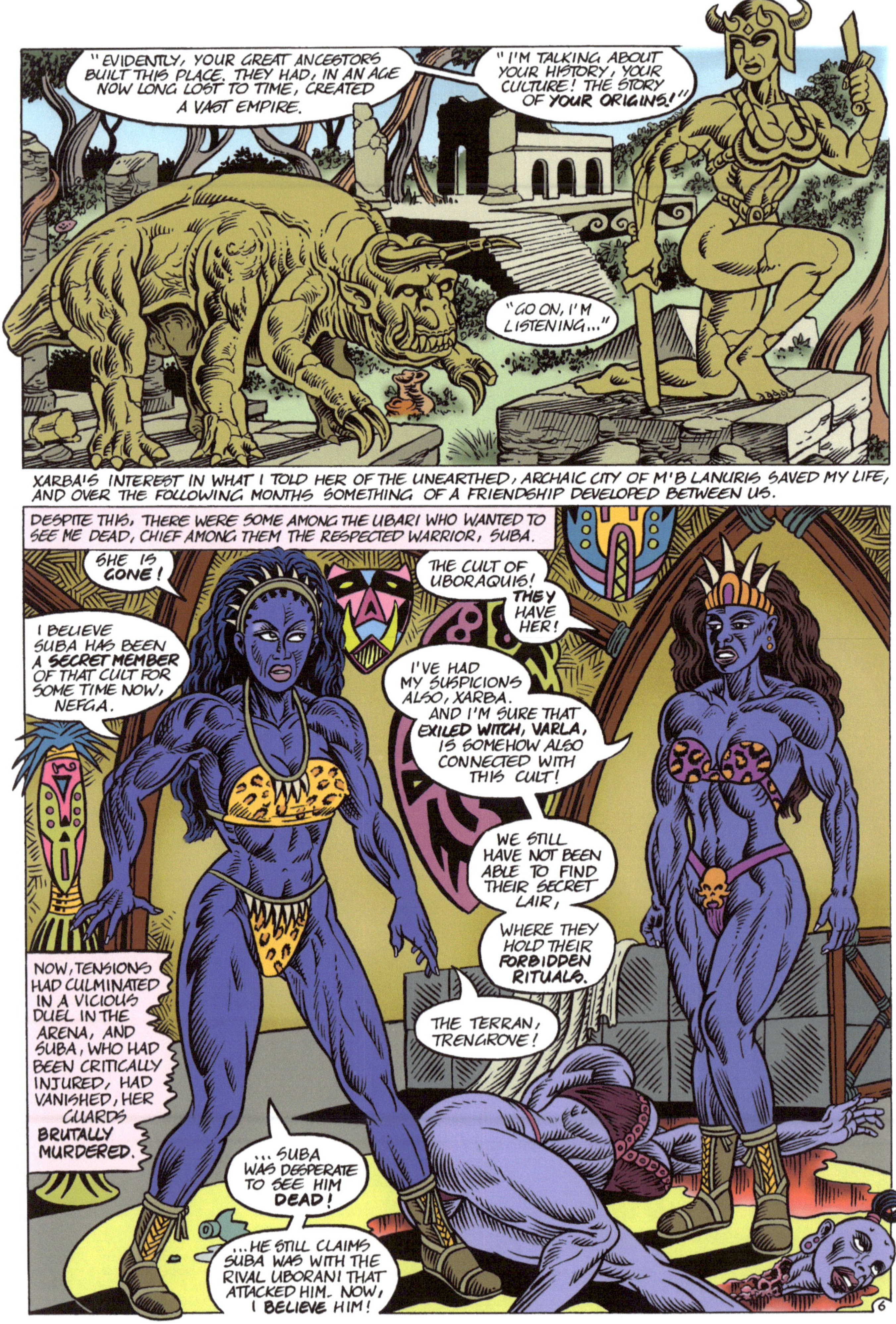

XARBA'S INTEREST IN WHAT I TOLD HER OF THE UNEARTHED, ARCHAIC CITY OF M'B LANURIS SAVED MY LIFE, AND OVER THE FOLLOWING MONTHS SOMETHING OF A FRIENDSHIP DEVELOPED BETWEEN US.

DESPITE THIS, THERE WERE SOME AMONG THE UBARI WHO WANTED TO SEE ME DEAD, CHIEF AMONG THEM THE RESPECTED WARRIOR, SUBA.

SHE IS GONE!

I BELIEVE SUBA HAS BEEN A SECRET MEMBER OF THAT CULT FOR SOME TIME NOW, NEFGA.

THE CULT OF UBORAQUIS! THEY HAVE HER!

I'VE HAD MY SUSPICIONS ALSO, XARBA. AND I'M SURE THAT EXILED WITCH, VARLA, IS SOMEHOW ALSO CONNECTED WITH THIS CULT!

WE STILL HAVE NOT BEEN ABLE TO FIND THEIR SECRET LAIR,

WHERE THEY HOLD THEIR FORBIDDEN RITUALS.

THE TERRAN, TRENGROVE!

NOW, TENSIONS HAD CULMINATED IN A VICIOUS DUEL IN THE ARENA, AND SUBA, WHO HAD BEEN CRITICALLY INJURED, HAD VANISHED, HER GUARDS BRUTALLY MURDERED.

...SUBA WAS DESPERATE TO SEE HIM DEAD!

...HE STILL CLAIMS SUBA WAS WITH THE RIVAL UBORANI THAT ATTACKED HIM. NOW, I BELIEVE HIM!

6

ELSEWHERE IN THE VALLEY, INSIDE AN ANCIENT TEMPLE,
YOU ARE MORTALLY WOUNDED, SUBA. IT IS TIME...
IF YOU WISH TO LIVE AND DELIVER VENGEANCE UPON THOSE WHO HAVE WRONGED YOU, YOU MUST BECOME ONE OF THE UBORAQUIS!
EAT OF THIS. THE POWER OF THE UBORAQUIS - ETERNAL DEVOURER OF ALL ENEMIES - WILL ENTER YOUR BODY AND SOUL!
I AM WILLING. I WILL DO IT!
"EAT ALL EXCEPT THE HEAD, SUBA."
YES!
SOME HOURS LATER,
YOU ARE NOW A FAR STRONGER WARRIOR THAN ANY UBORANI, SUBA. YOU ARE IMPERVIOUS TO WOUNDS THAT WOULD SLAY YOUR ENEMIES!
THE PAIN; THE WOUND! GONE!
I HUNGER! - FOR A MAN,
- FOR FLESH TO EAT!
YES, SUBA, TO KEEP UP YOUR STRENGTH YOU WILL NEED TO FEED, MORE THAN EVER BEFORE...
... BUT WITHOUT MY GUIDANCE, YOU WILL BE LOST. YOU MUST NEVER FORGET THAT, OR YOU WILL REGRESS INTO A BEAST-STATE, AND AS SUCH YOU WILL REMAIN!
I, VARLA, WARRIOR PRIESTESS OF THE UBORAQUIS WAR CULT, AM YOUR FRIEND AND PROTECTOR! I WILL LEAD YOU ALL TO VICTORY OVER YOUR ENEMIES!
XARBA AND HER ARROGANT DEVOTEES HAVE RULED THIS VALLEY FOR FAR TOO LONG!
TOGETHER WE HAVE PLOTTED AGAINST UBARI TYRANNY! NOW WE WILL FIGHT THE UBARI! XARBA AND THE FALSE PRIESTESS NEFGA SHALL DIE! ...ALL I REQUIRE IS YOUR LOYALTY, SUBA. I WILL SEE TO YOUR EVERY NEED. - BUT YOU MUST NEVER BETRAY ME.
YES! I SHALL KILL XARBA!
7

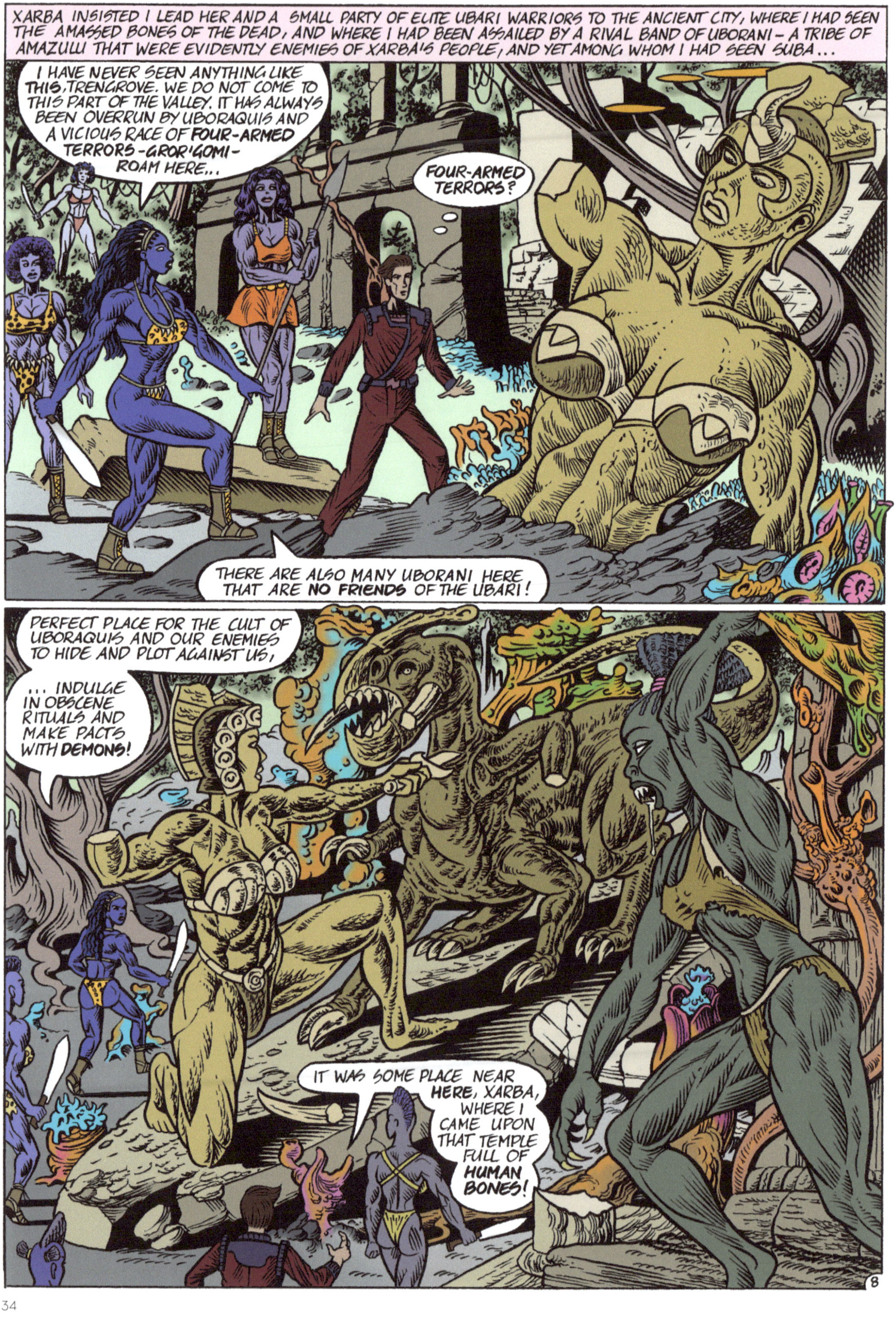

XARBA INSISTED I LEAD HER AND A SMALL PARTY OF ELITE UBARI WARRIORS TO THE ANCIENT CITY, WHERE I HAD SEEN THE AMASSED BONES OF THE DEAD, AND WHERE I HAD BEEN ASSAILED BY A RIVAL BAND OF UBORANI — A TRIBE OF AMAZULU THAT WERE EVIDENTLY ENEMIES OF XARBA'S PEOPLE, AND YET AMONG WHOM I HAD SEEN SUBA...

I HAVE NEVER SEEN ANYTHING LIKE THIS, TRENGROVE. WE DO NOT COME TO THIS PART OF THE VALLEY. IT HAS ALWAYS BEEN OVERRUN BY UBORAQUIS AND A VICIOUS RACE OF FOUR-ARMED TERRORS —GROR'GOMI— ROAM HERE...
FOUR-ARMED TERRORS?
THERE ARE ALSO MANY UBORANI HERE THAT ARE NO FRIENDS OF THE UBARI!

PERFECT PLACE FOR THE CULT OF UBORAQUIS AND OUR ENEMIES TO HIDE AND PLOT AGAINST US,
...INDULGE IN OBSCENE RITUALS AND MAKE PACTS WITH DEMONS!
IT WAS SOME PLACE NEAR HERE, XARBA, WHERE I CAME UPON THAT TEMPLE FULL OF HUMAN BONES!

8

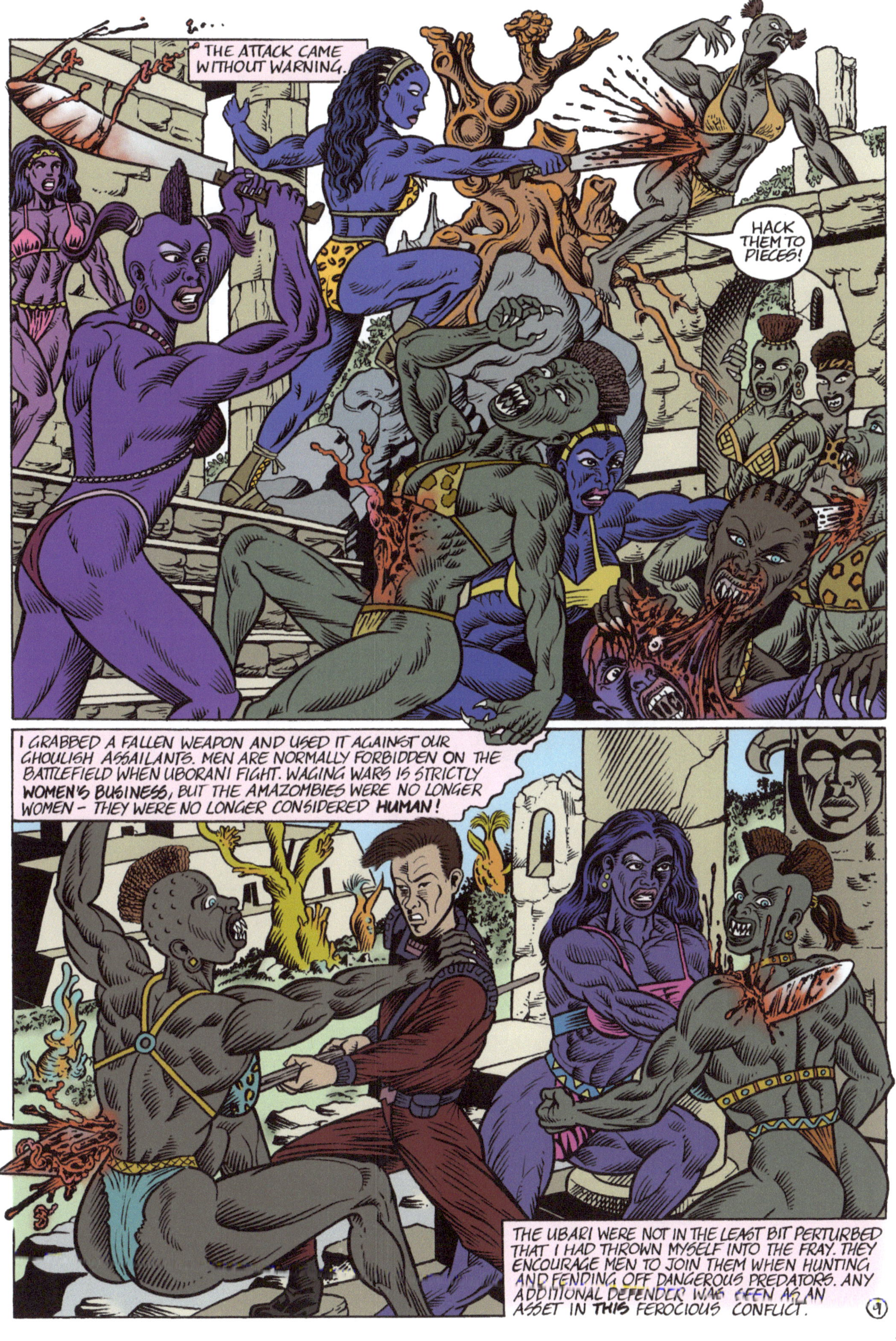

THE ATTACK CAME WITHOUT WARNING.
HACK THEM TO PIECES!
I GRABBED A FALLEN WEAPON AND USED IT AGAINST OUR GHOULISH ASSAILANTS. MEN ARE NORMALLY FORBIDDEN ON THE BATTLEFIELD WHEN UBORANI FIGHT. WAGING WARS IS STRICTLY WOMEN'S BUSINESS, BUT THE AMAZOMBIES WERE NO LONGER WOMEN — THEY WERE NO LONGER CONSIDERED HUMAN!
THE UBARI WERE NOT IN THE LEAST BIT PERTURBED THAT I HAD THROWN MYSELF INTO THE FRAY. THEY ENCOURAGE MEN TO JOIN THEM WHEN HUNTING AND FENDING OFF DANGEROUS PREDATORS. ANY ADDITIONAL DEFENDER WAS SEEN AS AN ASSET IN THIS FEROCIOUS CONFLICT.

TERRAN RESEARCH HAS REVEALED THAT THE UBORAQUIS DID NOT HAVE SUPERNATURAL ORIGINS. THEY ARE THE PRODUCT OF A UNIQUE VIRUS THAT IS TRANSMITTED WHEN LOCAL WOMEN—AND GROR'GOMI—CONSUME THE FLESH OF A SPECIFIC SPECIES OF REPTILES INDIGENOUS TO THE VALLEY OF M'B LANURIS.
THE VIRUS CAUSES MUTATION AND IS LINKED TO THE REPRODUCTIVE CYCLE OF THE REPTILES, WHICH HAVE NO GENDER.
THAT'S IT, XARBA!
THE TEMPLE FULL OF DEATH!
VARLA! THE BANISHED PRIESTESS, AND HER ACOLYTES, WHO HAD FLED WITH HER! SHE'S THE HIGH PRIESTESS OF THE CULT OF UBORAQUIS!
THAT PAIR!
...FOUR ARMED TERRORS! ARE THEY GROR'GOMI?
YES! BUT BECOME UBORAQUIS! ...SORCERY!
IT ALTERS THE DNA OF THE INFECTED WOMEN, WHO SUBSEQUENTLY PRODUCE REPTILIAN OFFSPRING INSTEAD OF HUMAN BABIES.
UBORAQUIS —AMAZOMBIES— INHERIT ADVANCED REGENERATIVE POWERS, AND LIKE THE REPTILES THAT INFECTED THEM, CAN REGENERATE SEVERED LIMBS AND QUICKLY RECOVER FROM TRAUMATIC INJURIES.
10

AS THE VESSELS THAT PRODUCE NEW GENERATIONS OF REPTILES, THESE ATTRIBUTES SIGNIFICANTLY INCREASE THEIR CHANCES OF SURVIVAL. FUELING THEIR HEIGHTENED METABOLISM IS THEIR RAPACIOUS NEED FOR FLESH. THEIR SEXUAL DESIRE IS ALSO INTENSIFIED, ASSURING THEY KEEP REPRODUCING.
THERE HAVE ALWAYS BEEN UBORAQUIS LURKING IN THE FOREST, BUT IT WAS VARLA WHO CREATED THIS CULT AS A MEANS OF DESTROYING THE UBARI!
KILL VARLA,
KILL THE CULT!

UBORANI WOMEN ARE ESPECIALLY SUSCEPTIBLE TO THE VIRUS AND THE REPTILES EMIT PHEROMONES THAT INDUCE A POWERFUL HUNGER URGE WHENEVER THEY ARE WITHIN THE PROXIMITY OF ANY WOMAN.
IF ONLY A FEW WOMEN SUCCUMB TO THE PHEROMONE'S EFFECTS EACH TIME IT IS RELEASED, THIS REPTILIAN SPECIES' SURVIVAL IS ASSURED.

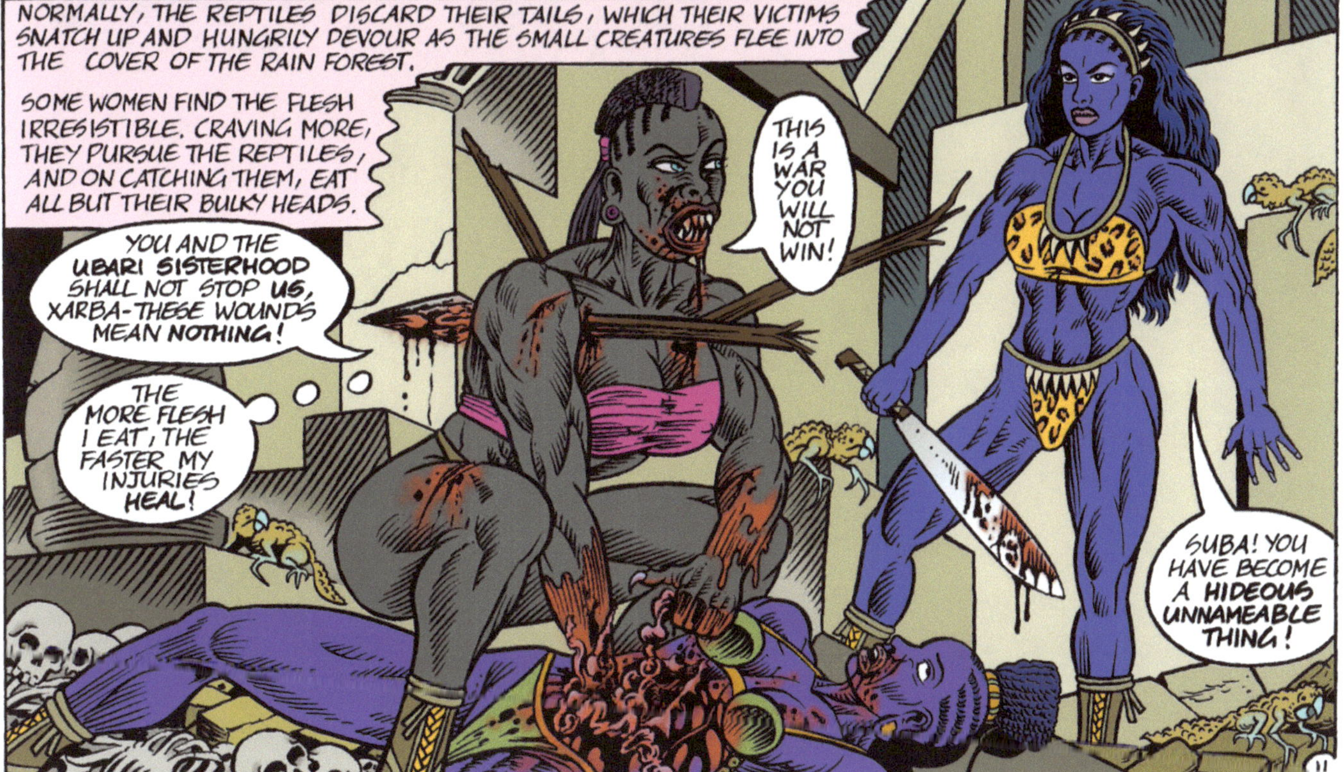

NORMALLY, THE REPTILES DISCARD THEIR TAILS, WHICH THEIR VICTIMS SNATCH UP AND HUNGRILY DEVOUR AS THE SMALL CREATURES FLEE INTO THE COVER OF THE RAIN FOREST.
SOME WOMEN FIND THE FLESH IRRESISTIBLE. CRAVING MORE, THEY PURSUE THE REPTILES, AND ON CATCHING THEM, EAT ALL BUT THEIR BULKY HEADS.
YOU AND THE UBARI SISTERHOOD SHALL NOT STOP US, XARBA—THESE WOUNDS MEAN NOTHING!
THE MORE FLESH I EAT, THE FASTER MY INJURIES HEAL!
THIS IS A WAR YOU WILL NOT WIN!
SUBA! YOU HAVE BECOME A HIDEOUS UNNAMEABLE THING!

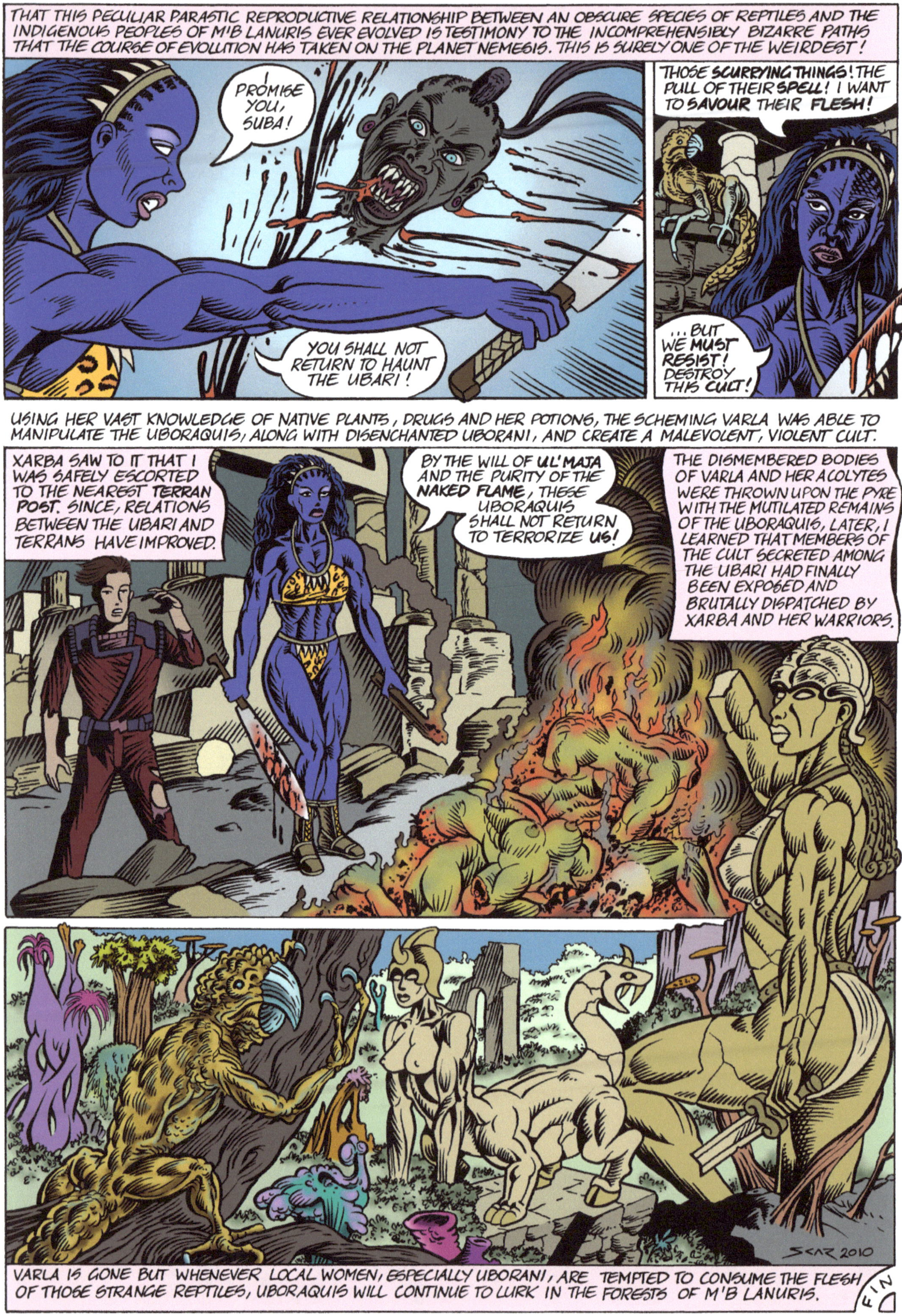

THAT THIS PECULIAR PARASTIC REPRODUCTIVE RELATIONSHIP BETWEEN AN OBSCURE SPECIES OF REPTILES AND THE INDIGENOUS PEOPLES OF M'B LANURIS EVER EVOLVED IS TESTIMONY TO THE INCOMPREHENSIBLY BIZARRE PATHS THAT THE COURSE OF EVOLUTION HAS TAKEN ON THE PLANET NEMESIS. THIS IS SURELY ONE OF THE WEIRDEST!

USING HER VAST KNOWLEDGE OF NATIVE PLANTS, DRUGS AND HER POTIONS, THE SCHEMING VARLA WAS ABLE TO MANIPULATE THE UBORAQUIS, ALONG WITH DISENCHANTED UBORANI, AND CREATE A MALEVOLENT, VIOLENT CULT.

XARBA SAW TO IT THAT I WAS SAFELY ESCORTED TO THE NEAREST TERRAN POST. SINCE, RELATIONS BETWEEN THE UBARI AND TERRANS HAVE IMPROVED.

THE DISMEMBERED BODIES OF VARLA AND HER ACOLYTES WERE THROWN UPON THE PYRE WITH THE MUTILATED REMAINS OF THE UBORAQUIS, LATER, I LEARNED THAT MEMBERS OF THE CULT SECRETED AMONG THE UBARI HAD FINALLY BEEN EXPOSED AND BRUTALLY DISPATCHED BY XARBA AND HER WARRIORS.

VARLA IS GONE BUT WHENEVER LOCAL WOMEN, ESPECIALLY UBORANI, ARE TEMPTED TO CONSUME THE FLESH OF THOSE STRANGE REPTILES, UBORAQUIS WILL CONTINUE TO LURK IN THE FORESTS OF M'B LANURIS.

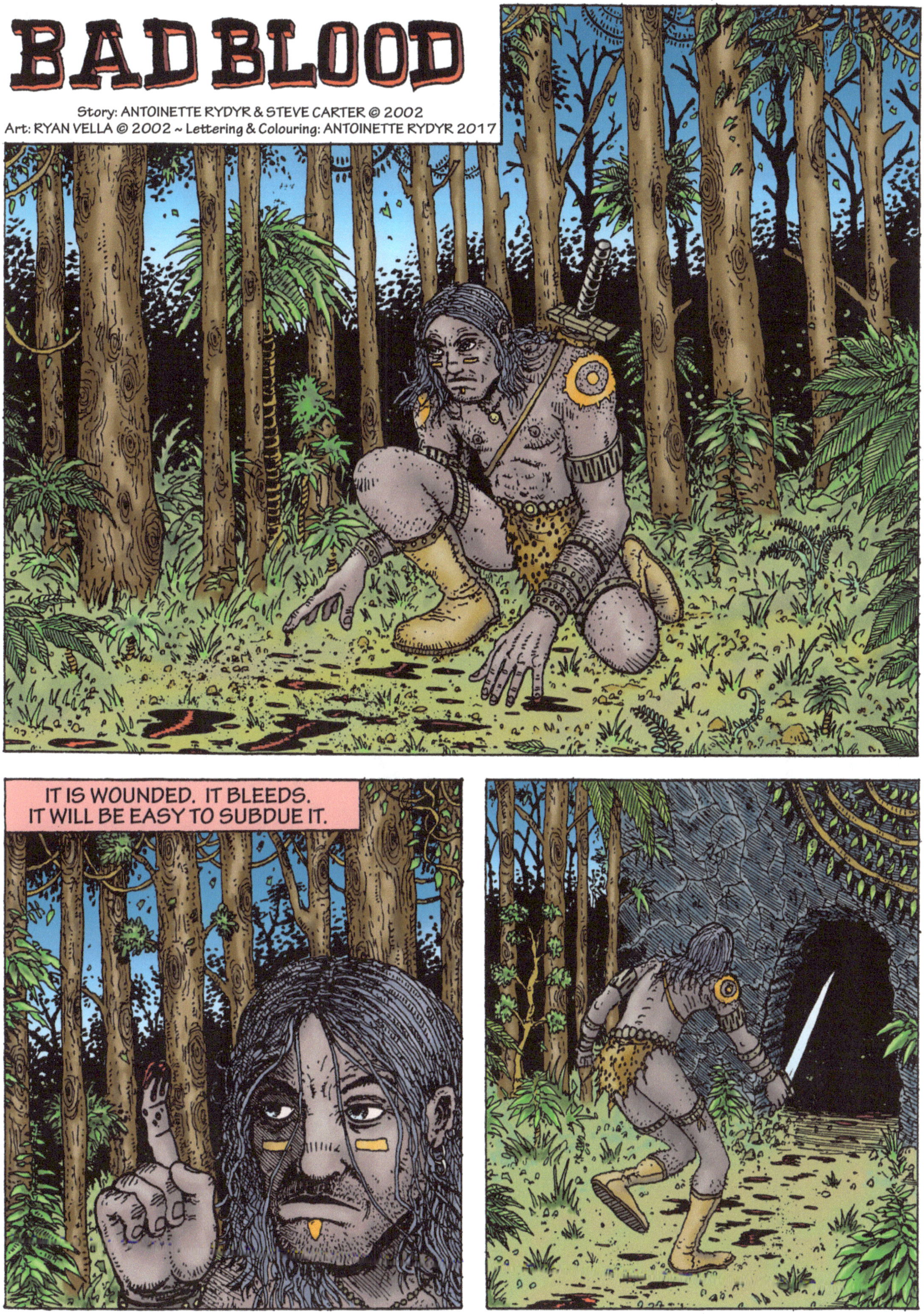

BAD BLOOD

Story: ANTOINETTE RYDYR & STEVE CARTER © 2002
Art: RYAN VELLA © 2002 ~ Lettering & Colouring: ANTOINETTE RYDYR 2017

SEE, IT COWERS IN PAIN. IT SURELY DOES NOT HAVE LONG TO LIVE. I WILL HASTEN ITS DEMISE.

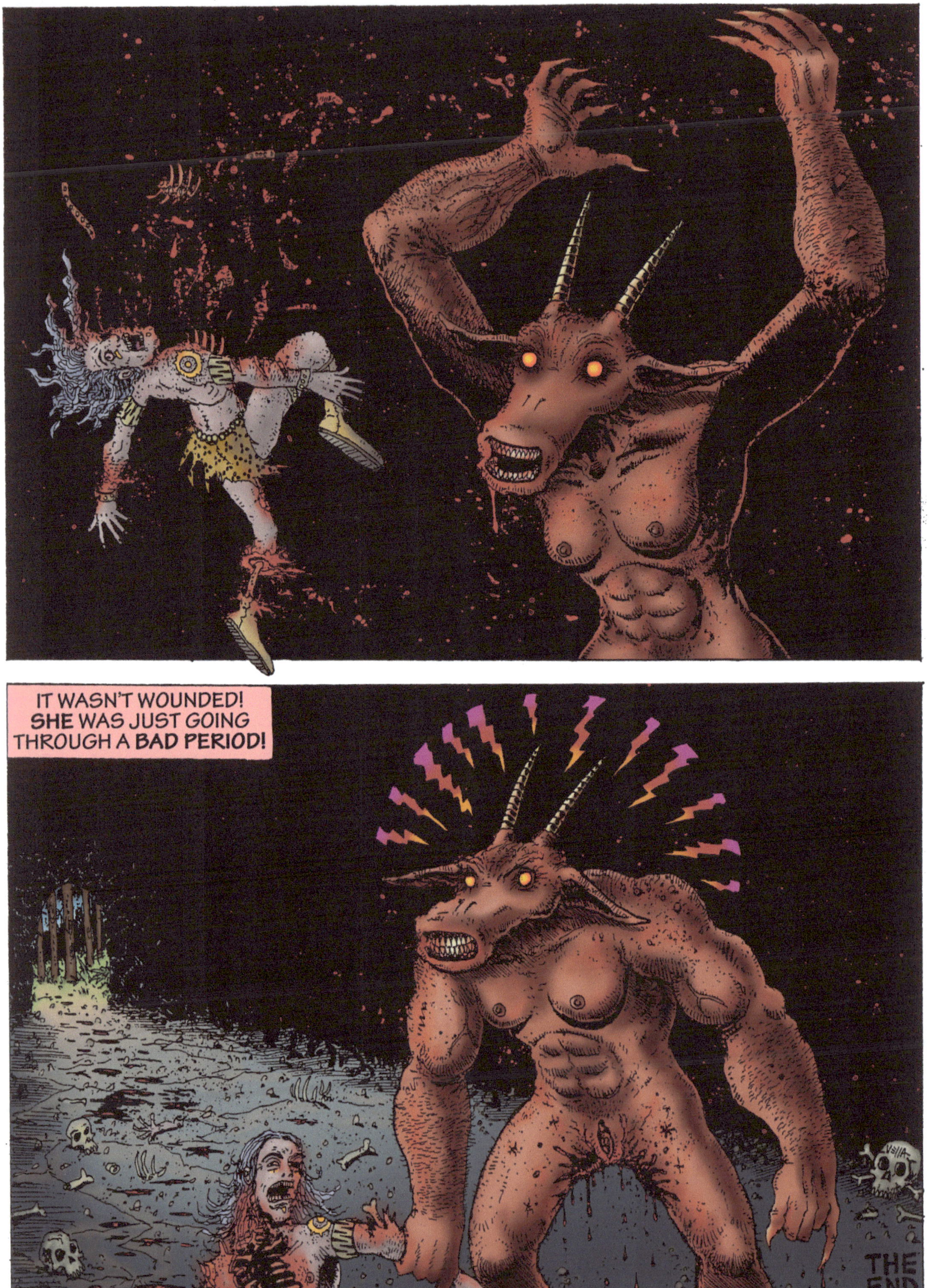

IT WASN'T WOUNDED!
SHE WAS JUST GOING
THROUGH A BAD PERIOD!
THE END

SKIN
DEEP

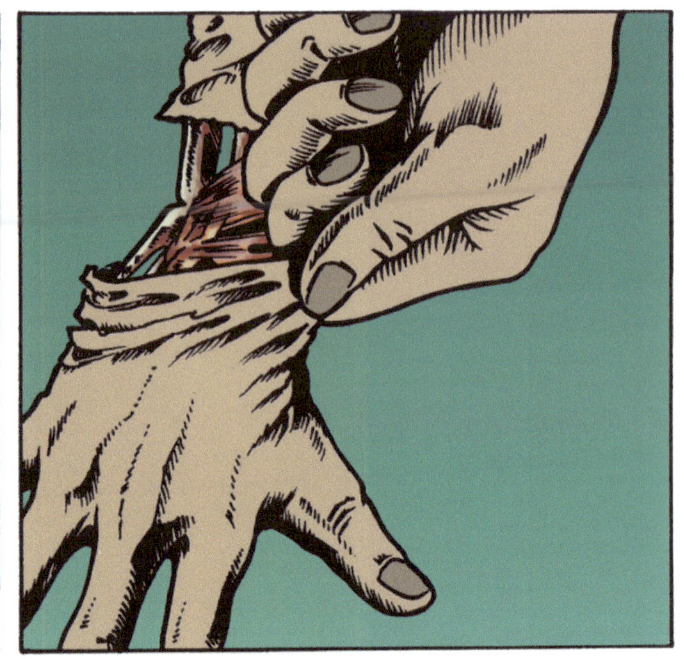

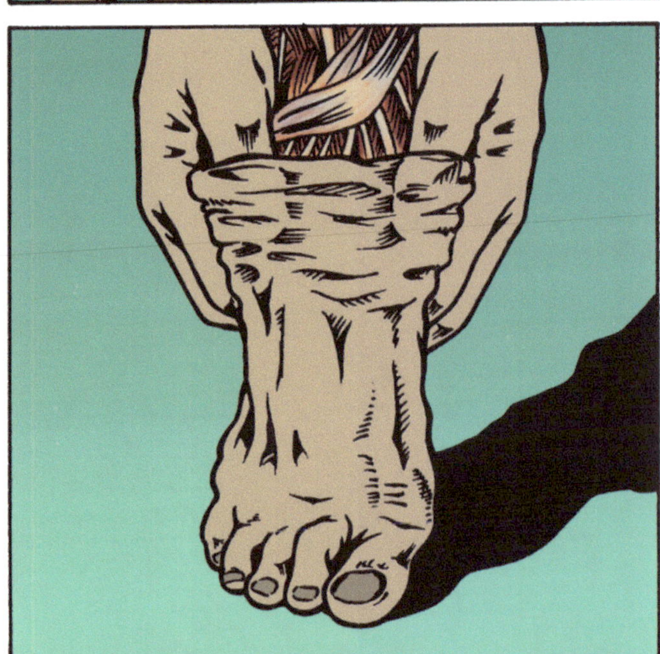

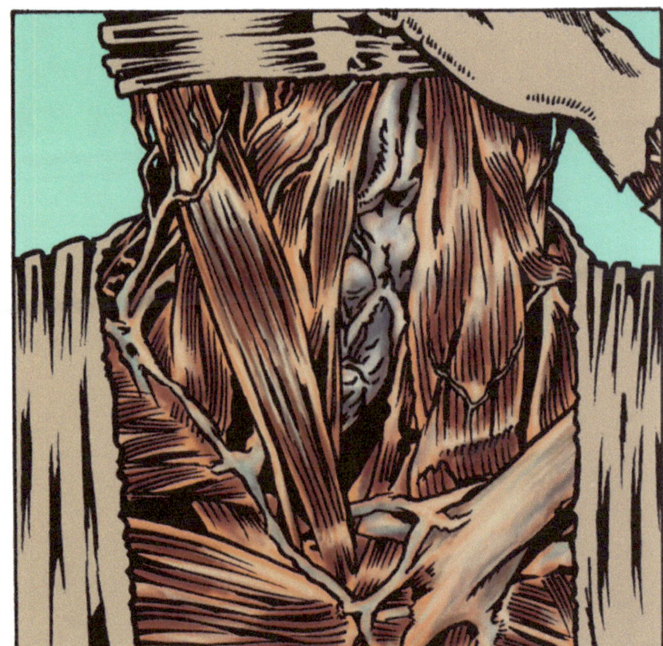

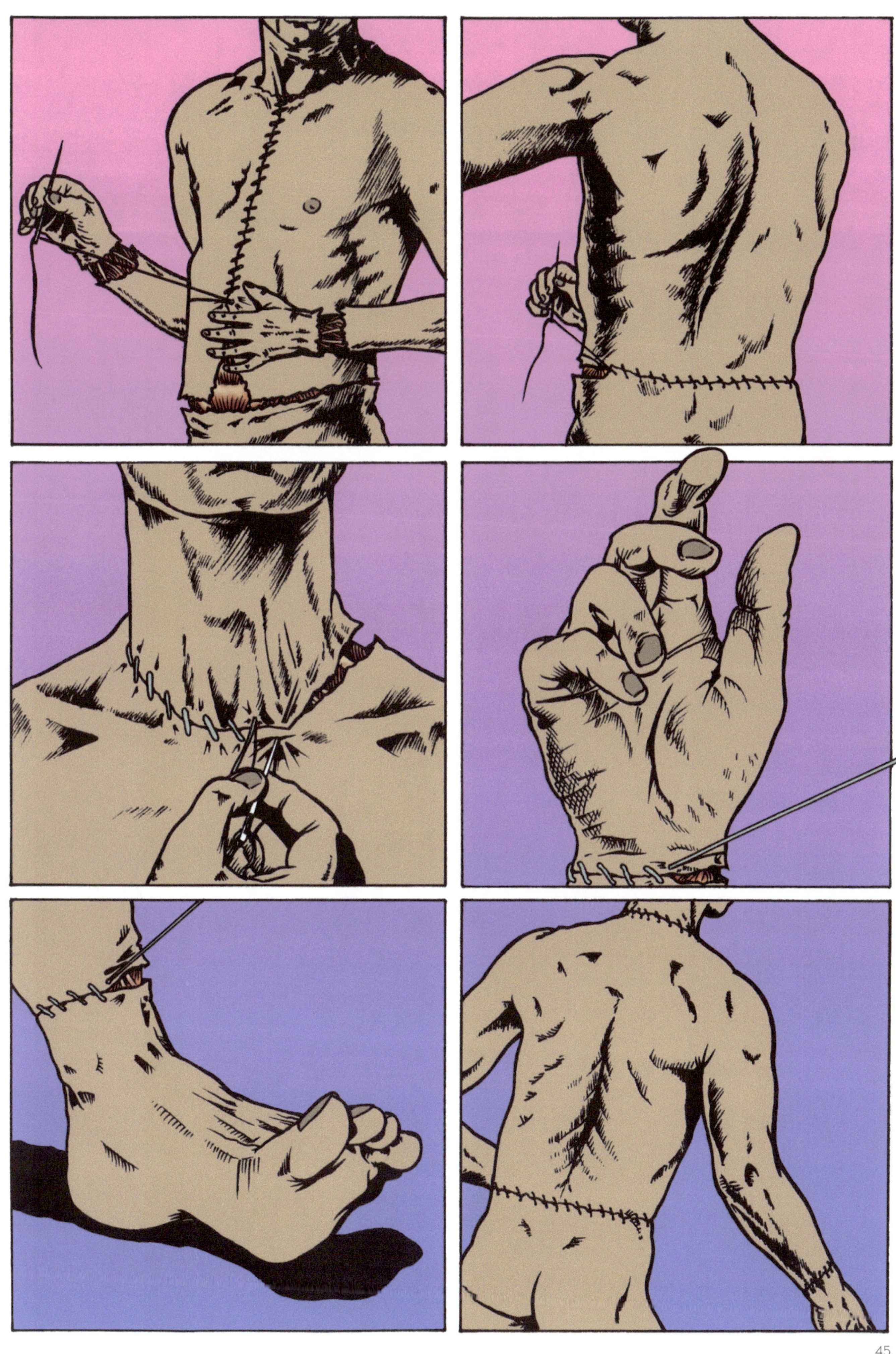

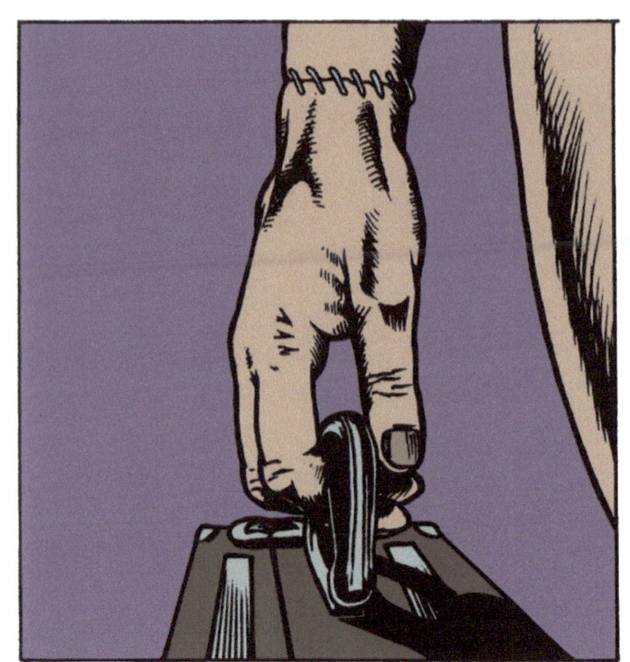

Lucas and Bundy
Associates at Law.

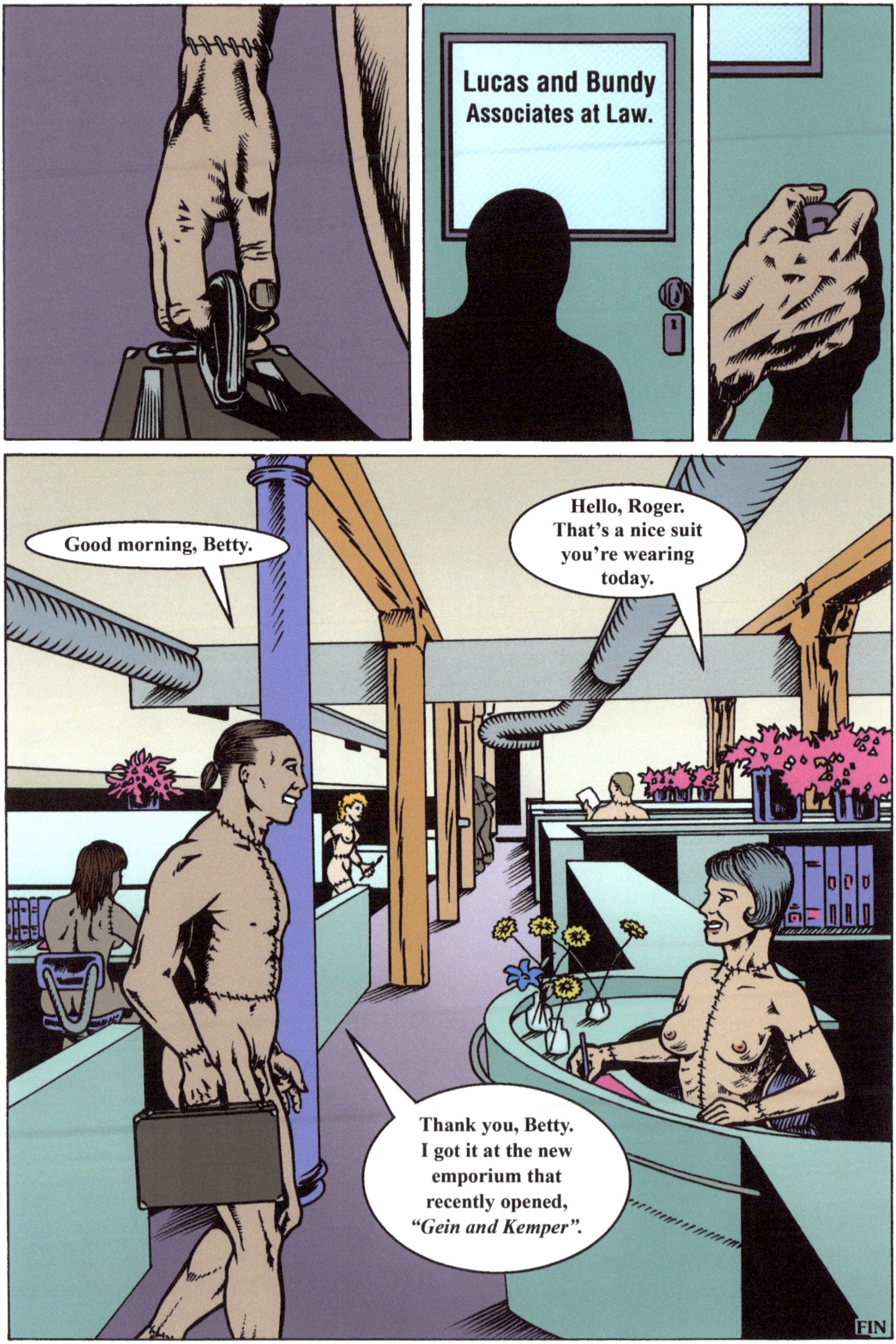

Good morning, Betty.
Hello, Roger. That's a nice suit you're wearing today.
Thank you, Betty. I got it at the new emporium that recently opened, "Gein and Kemper".
FIN

SEEDS of DEATH

MOST OF THE SEEDS FALL TO THE GROUND WHERE THEY'LL EVENTUALLY SHRIVEL AND DIE, BUT A FEW LAND UPON THE BACK OF ONE OF THE HURGULODONS, WHICH CONTINUES TO GRAZE, UNAWARE OF THEIR PRESENCE.

THE TINY SEEDS IMMEDIATELY SEND SHOOTS INTO THE UNWARY SUBHUMAN BRUTE'S HIDE.

SOON THEY WILL ROOT THEMSELVES DEEP INTO THE CREATURE AND FEED OFF ITS BLOOD...

OVER TIME, THE ONCE POWERFUL BULL-HURGULODON FELL ILL, ITS GREAT STRENGTH HAVING GRADUALLY BEING DRAINED BY THE PARASITIC PLANTS GROWING WITHIN. EVENTUALLY, THE DAY CAME WHEN A NEW GENERATION OF THE SEEDS OF DEATH SPROUTED FROM ITS DECAYING CARCASS.

COLOURS:
P. CORREY 2017

S. CARTER
+
A. ZYDYR
© 1993
2010

MORTAL MAN LIVES FOR ONLY A SHORT TIME,
. . . BUT DEMONS ARE FOREVER.
THE WELL OF SOULS
© 2004 SCARGS
SCRIPT & PENCILS: STEVE CARTER & ANTOINETTE RYDYR
INKS: GLENN SMITH
COLOURS & LETTERING: ANTOINETTE RYDYR 2017
Based on the story "Hell Whores of Chaos" by Steve Carter and Antoinette Rydyr 2004

FRESH FROM THE TRAUMA OF DEATH. . . . CONFUSED, DISORIENTATED, NO DOUBT. I SEE YOUR FORMER LIFE MADE LITTLE IMPACT, ON YOU OR ANYBODY ELSE. A SOMEWHAT LAZY LOAFER AND A BIT OF A SPONGER, THAT ABOUT SUMS YOU UP, DAVID MAYFIELD . . .
NO, NO, NO! THIS IS NOT MAKING ANY SENSE!

IN FACT, IT'S DOWNRIGHT CRAZY! SOME WOMAN IN A MEDIEVAL OUTFIT MAKING SNIDE REMARKS ABOUT ME, THAT I COULD WELL DO WITHOUT . . . WHAT'S IT ALL S'POSED TO MEAN?

NEVER MARRIED, NOT EVEN A COMMON LAW WIFE TO MOURN YOUR PASSING. NOT VERY LUCKY IN MATTERS OF LOVE WERE YOU?
MY NAME IS MEDINA AND I AM YOUR DESTINY.
THIS'S TOO MUCH! NOW IT'S MY PERSONAL LIFE!
WHO ARE YOU, LADY? WHAT DO YOU WANT WITH ME?
I BROUGHT YOU HERE.

WHAT ARE YOU TALKING ABOUT? AND WHERE AND WHAT IS "HERE"?
THIS IS A WELL, INTO WHICH SOULS FALL AND ARE COLLECTED. IT IS WE WHO DETERMINE WHOSE SOULS COME HERE, AND WE WHO TAKE RESPONSIBILITY FOR EVERY LAST ONE.
YOU'VE HIJACKED ME, MY SOUL! THAT'S WHAT YOU'RE SAYING.
THAT'S ONE WAY TO SEE IT.
THEN AGAIN YOU'D BE LOST WITHOUT ME.

THIS IS JUST ONE OF AN INFINITE NUMBER OF WELLS, SPREAD THROUGHOUT A VAST DOMAIN WHICH STRETCHES ACROSS ETERNITY.
THIS IS WHERE YOU ARE NOW . . .
ETERNITY, INFINITY, FOREVER.
. . . SOMETHING YOU SHOULD CONTEMPLATE. IT'S YOUR FATE.

COME, YOU HAVE TO SEE THIS.
WHAT IS MAKING THAT TERRIBLE DIN?
IN JUST A MOMENT, YOU WILL SEE.

TWO GREAT ARMIES!
YES, LOCKED IN ETERNAL COMBAT . . .
WE ARE ONE OF THEM.
CALL IT THE APOCALYPSE, ARMAGEDDON, RAGNAROK . . .
THERE ARE MANY NAMES FOR IT.

CAN YOU SEE WHAT IT IS THAT WE FIGHT?

THEY DON'T LOOK HUMAN. WHO, WHAT, ARE THEY?

THEY ARE KNOWN BY MANY NAMES. BACK IN THAT POCKET UNIVERSE YOU HAVE SO RECENTLY DEPARTED, EVERY TIME THE SEED OF A MAN OR BOY DOES NOT FIND ITS WAY INTO THE WOMB OF A WOMAN AND CREATES A NEW SOUL, ONE OF THEM ~ A CHAOS WITCH ~ COMES INTO EXISTENCE.

THEY ARE THE LASCIVIOUS MANIFESTATION OF ALL LUST AND MASTURBATION. HOW MANY CHAOS WITCHES DO YOU THINK THAT YOU ALONE CAN ACCOUNT FOR?

... NOW THINK OF EVERY MAN OR BOY WHO EVER LIVED.

OKAY, OKAY! I GET THE PICTURE!

THAT SHOULD GIVE YOU AN IDEA OF JUST HOW MANY OF THEM THERE ARE.

... AND YOU'RE BLAMING ME?

YOU ARE BUT ONE SMALL CONTRIBUTOR TO THE PROBLEM.

BUT YOU DO NEED TO KNOW ABOUT SEXUAL RELATIONS IN THIS REALM ... THE MALE STILL GIVES, FEMALES RECEIVE. ENERGY IS TRANSFERRED FROM THE MALE TO THE FEMALE DURING COITUS.

... AND THEY OUT THERE, THE CHAOS WITCHES, THEY'RE INSATIABLE. YOU'LL BE DRAINED, WHITHER ...

THEY ARE NOTHING COMPARED TO WHAT IS CREATED EVERY TIME A RAPE, ANY ACT OF BRUTALITY OR MURDER IS COMMITTED.

I DON'T WANT TO KNOW.

YOU NEED NOT BE CONCERNED ABOUT THAT ...

WE ARE ALL THAT STANDS BETWEEN YOU, THIS SOUL WELL AND THAT HORDE OF CHAOS WITCHES OUTSIDE.
YOU'RE SAYING THOSE THINGS ARE AFTER ME?! ...AND THIS WELL?
THEY WANT THIS WELL AND DOMINION OVER EVERY MALE IN IT.
...YOUR SOUL WILL BELONG TO THEM.
THEY'LL FEED OFF ME,
DEVOUR MY SOUL!
I WILL THEN BE FINALLY, TRULY DEAD! THAT'S WHAT YOU'RE TELLING ME?
NO, NOT QUITE. YOUR SOUL IS IMMORTAL, BUT YOU WILL BECOME INCREDIBLY WEAK, EVEN UNABLE TO MOVE.
THEY'LL KEEP YOU IN A STATE OF PERPETUAL LETHARGY, CONSTANTLY SYPHONING OFF YOUR SOUL.
THAT IS WHAT THEY CRAVE.
THAT BATTLE OUT THERE...
THE MAIMING, THE KILLING...
NOTHING HERE DIES. YOU, WE, THEM. THE PAIN, ALL SENSATIONS ARE REAL FOR US ALL.
THE DEATH TRAUMA CAN BE EXPERIENCED OVER AND AGAIN, BUT RECOVERY IS SLOW, AGONISING.
THIS IS ETERNITY, EXISTING IN INFINITY. IT GOES ON FOREVER.
WHAT'S THE POINT?
WE CAN'T LET THEM WIN. THEY ARE DETERMINED TO WIN. THIS IS JUST ONE BATTLE IN AN ENDLESS WAR THAT MUST BE FOUGHT.
...IT'S INSANE!
...AND THIS IS ALL LEADING WHERE?
...TO THE REASON YOU ARE HERE. IF WE ARE TO STOP THE CHAOS WITCHES FROM DOMINATING THIS REALM WE MUST HAVE A CONSTANT ENERGY SUPPLY.
YOU CONTRIBUTED TO THEIR CREATION.
IT'S ONLY FAIR THAT YOU PLAY YOUR PART IN HELPING TO REDRESS THE BALANCE.
4

NOW, WAIT A MINUTE!
I'M OFFERING YOU TWO THINGS YOU NEVER HAD IN YOUR PREVIOUS EXISTENCE,
A STABLE JOB AND PLENTY OF ATTENTION FROM ATTRACTIVE WOMEN.
IN RETURN WE'LL BE THE GUARDIANS OF YOUR SOUL.
THIS'S GETTING MORE ABSURD BY THE MINUTE.
SOMETHING'S NOT RIGHT HERE. DAMNED IF I KNOW WHAT, THOUGH.
THIS PAIR DON'T LOOK HAPPY,
CAN'T IMAGINE YOU'D REFUSE SUCH A GENEROUS OFFER. ACTUALLY, YOU'RE IN NO POSITION TO REFUSE,
IT'S SIMPLY NOT AN OPTION.
THIS'S OUTRAGEOUS!
YOU'LL LOVE IT HERE.
ALL MEN DO! PERFECTLY SUITED TO YOUR NEEDS.
YOU'VE NEVER HAD IT SO GOOD.
A SOUL SNATCHER!
!?
SHE WANTS YOU, WANTS TO TAKE YOU TO THE CHAOS WITCHES. BUT ONLY AFTER SHE IS FINISHED WITH YOU!
APOCALYPSE HARPIES!
MEN ATTRACT THEM LIKE FLIES!
THAT IS WHY ALL MEN MUST STAY WITHIN THE CITADEL, UNLESS YOU PREFER HER COMPANY TO OURS.
5

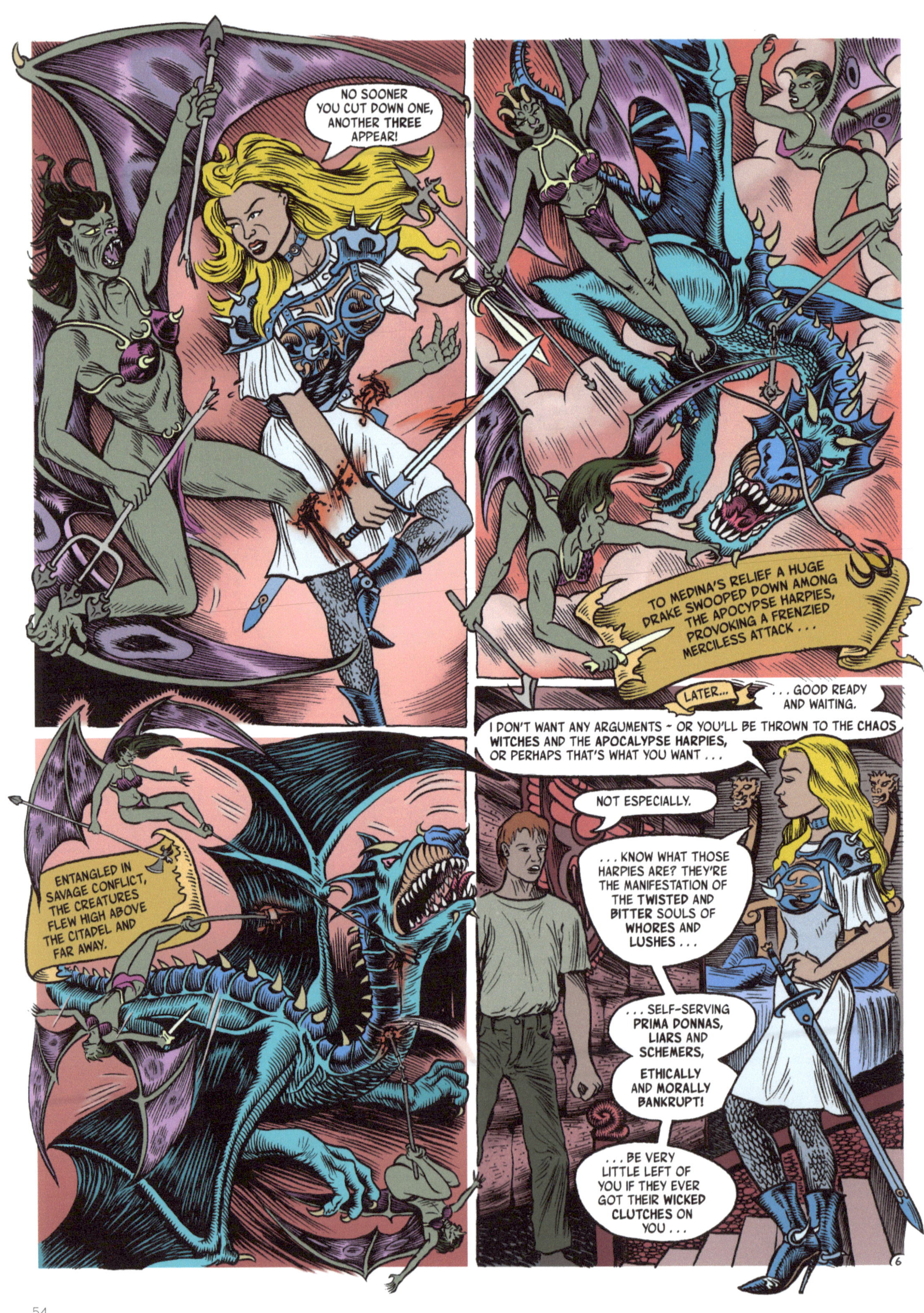
NO SOONER YOU CUT DOWN ONE, ANOTHER THREE APPEAR!
TO MEDINA'S RELIEF A HUGE DRAKE SWOOPED DOWN AMONG THE APOCYPSE HARPIES, PROVOKING A FRENZIED MERCILESS ATTACK . . .
ENTANGLED IN SAVAGE CONFLICT, THE CREATURES FLEW HIGH ABOVE THE CITADEL AND FAR AWAY.
LATER . . .
. . . GOOD READY AND WAITING.
I DON'T WANT ANY ARGUMENTS ~ OR YOU'LL BE THROWN TO THE CHAOS WITCHES AND THE APOCALYPSE HARPIES, OR PERHAPS THAT'S WHAT YOU WANT . . .
NOT ESPECIALLY.
. . . KNOW WHAT THOSE HARPIES ARE? THEY'RE THE MANIFESTATION OF THE TWISTED AND BITTER SOULS OF WHORES AND LUSHES . . .
. . . SELF-SERVING PRIMA DONNAS, LIARS AND SCHEMERS,
ETHICALLY AND MORALLY BANKRUPT!
. . . BE VERY LITTLE LEFT OF YOU IF THEY EVER GOT THEIR WICKED CLUTCHES ON YOU . . .
6

MEANWHILE, WITHIN A DEEP, SUBTERRANEAN STYGIAN CORRIDOR...
DO NOT TOUCH ME, YOU HELLWHORES! I FORBID IT!
A MISOGYNIST AND A CRUEL THUG! ...NOBODY CARES WHAT FATE AWAITS YOU!
SHUT UP!
SUFFER THE PROGENY OF YOUR ACTIONS!
THEY ARE THE ONLY ONES WHO HAVE NEED FOR YOU HERE...
WE HAVE BROUGHT YOU WHAT YOU DESIRE AND WHAT IS RIGHTFULLY YOURS, LAMIA.
WE ASK IN RETURN ONLY THAT YOU MAINTAIN THE SPELL.
GIVE US WHAT IS OURS,
AND ALL THAT IS,
...WILL REMAIN AS IS...
FOR NOW, WE CAN MEET YOUR DEMANDS. WE HAVE ACCESS TO THOSE OFF WHOM YOU MOST READILY FEED. OTHERWISE, THE PICKINGS WOULD BE THIN INDEED.
...SO YOU KEEP SAYING CHAOS WITCH.
WE WILL HONOUR THIS BOGUS ALLIANCE FOR NOW BUT THERE ARE NO GUARANTEES FOR HOW LONG IT CAN ENDURE. THAT IS SOMETHING BEYOND OUR CONTROL. IT TAKES MORE THAN SIMPLE WILLPOWER FOR US TO DO THIS. IT REQUIRES A MASSIVE AMOUNT OF ENERGY.
AND DARE I SAY IT, YOU CERTAINLY USE THEM UP QUICKLY ENOUGH!
BE THAT AS IT MAY. BUT REMEMBER YOU CANNOT DECEIVE US AS EASILY AS YOU CAN VEIL THE SENSES OF MERE MEN AND THE LESSER DEMONS AND BEASTS, LAMIA, AND YOU KNOW IT!
AS LONG AS YOU WILL IT, THE SPELL WILL REMAIN.
IT IS NOT MUCH TO ASK OF YOU CONSIDERING THE BANQUET YOU RECEIVE FROM US IN RETURN...
JUST KEEP BRINGING THEM TO US. ...THAT'S ALL YOU HAVE TO DO.
7

THAT DREAM! I'M WASTED!
SOMETHING'S DEFINITELY WRONG HERE . . .
. . . THE WOMAN, MEDINA, AND THE REST OF THEM . . .
THEY'RE THE DEMONS!
THAT'S GOT TO BE IT!
GOT TO GET OUT OF HERE!

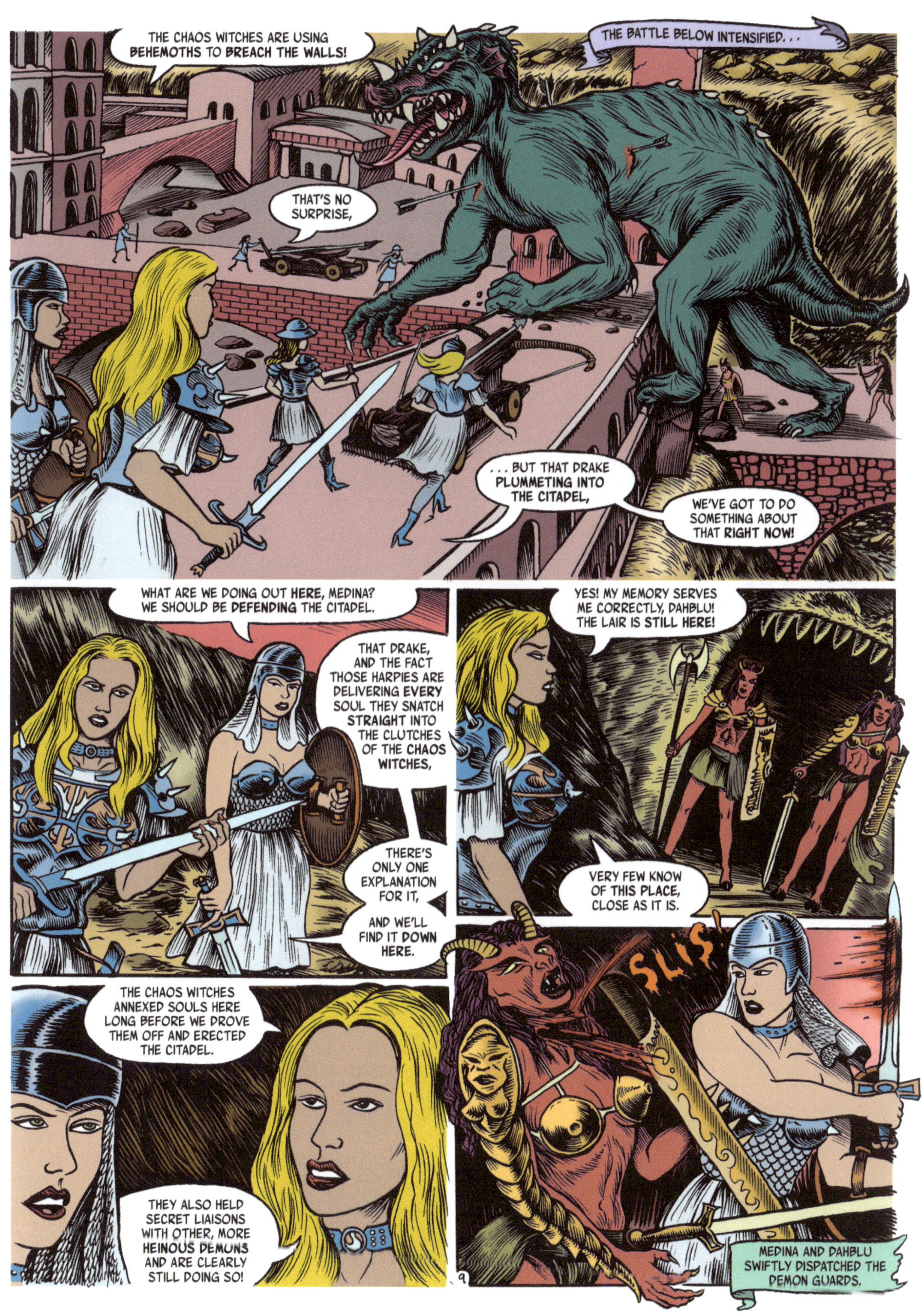

THE CHAOS WITCHES ARE USING BEHEMOTHS TO BREACH THE WALLS!
THE BATTLE BELOW INTENSIFIED...
THAT'S NO SURPRISE,
...BUT THAT DRAKE PLUMMETING INTO THE CITADEL,
WE'VE GOT TO DO SOMETHING ABOUT THAT RIGHT NOW!
WHAT ARE WE DOING OUT HERE, MEDINA? WE SHOULD BE DEFENDING THE CITADEL.
THAT DRAKE, AND THE FACT THOSE HARPIES ARE DELIVERING EVERY SOUL THEY SNATCH STRAIGHT INTO THE CLUTCHES OF THE CHAOS WITCHES,
THERE'S ONLY ONE EXPLANATION FOR IT,
AND WE'LL FIND IT DOWN HERE.
YES! MY MEMORY SERVES ME CORRECTLY, DAHBLU! THE LAIR IS STILL HERE!
VERY FEW KNOW OF THIS PLACE, CLOSE AS IT IS.
SLISH
THE CHAOS WITCHES ANNEXED SOULS HERE LONG BEFORE WE DROVE THEM OFF AND ERECTED THE CITADEL.
THEY ALSO HELD SECRET LIAISONS WITH OTHER, MORE HEINOUS DEMONS AND ARE CLEARLY STILL DOING SO!
MEDINA AND DAHBLU SWIFTLY DISPATCHED THE DEMON GUARDS.

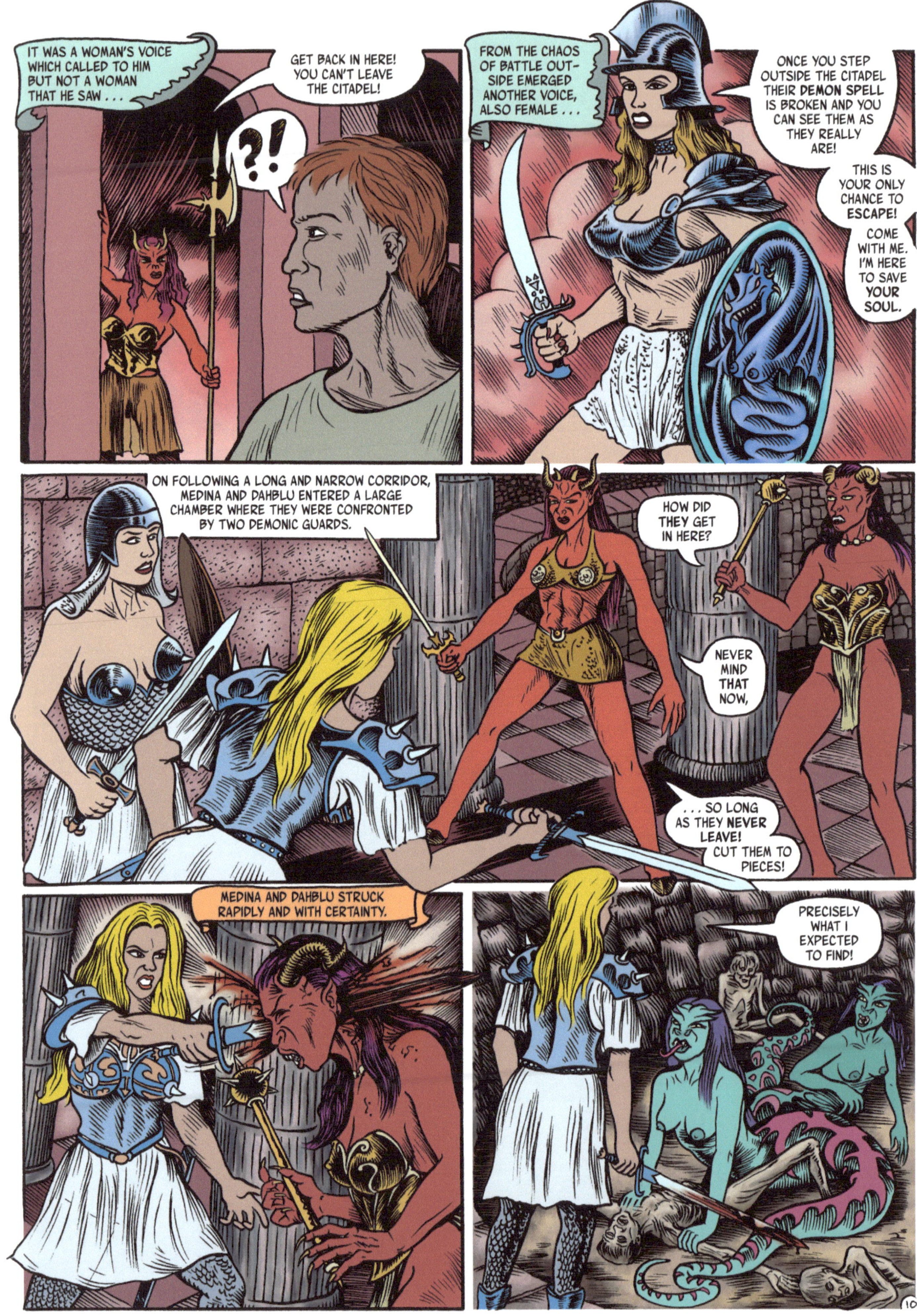

IT WAS A WOMAN'S VOICE WHICH CALLED TO HIM BUT NOT A WOMAN THAT HE SAW . . .
?!
GET BACK IN HERE! YOU CAN'T LEAVE THE CITADEL!
FROM THE CHAOS OF BATTLE OUTSIDE EMERGED ANOTHER VOICE, ALSO FEMALE . . .
ONCE YOU STEP OUTSIDE THE CITADEL THEIR DEMON SPELL IS BROKEN AND YOU CAN SEE THEM AS THEY REALLY ARE!
THIS IS YOUR ONLY CHANCE TO ESCAPE!
COME WITH ME. I'M HERE TO SAVE YOUR SOUL.
ON FOLLOWING A LONG AND NARROW CORRIDOR, MEDINA AND DAHBLU ENTERED A LARGE CHAMBER WHERE THEY WERE CONFRONTED BY TWO DEMONIC GUARDS.
HOW DID THEY GET IN HERE?
NEVER MIND THAT NOW,
. . . SO LONG AS THEY NEVER LEAVE! CUT THEM TO PIECES!
MEDINA AND DAHBLU STRUCK RAPIDLY AND WITH CERTAINTY.
PRECISELY WHAT I EXPECTED TO FIND!
10

YOU'RE SPELL IS BROKEN WITCH!
NOW THAT THE CHAOS WITCHES ARE FORCED TO RELY ONLY ON THEIR COMBAT SKILLS THEY'LL SOON FIND THEY ARE NO MATCH FOR US.
THEIR SEIGE WILL INEVITABLY FAIL!
WHAT IN HELL?!
THAT'S EXACTLY WHERE SHE WAS GOING TO TAKE YOU!
ONCE THE DEMONIC SPELL WAS BROKEN WHAT HAD APPEARED AS A WOMAN WAS EXPOSED AS A DEMON AND WAS PROMPTLY, BRUTALLY IMPALED.

THE DEMONIC HORDE OF CHAOS WITCHES WAS FINALLY FORCED TO RETREAT.
LATER, WITHIN A GLOOMY CHAMBER DEEP WITHIN THE CITADEL . . .
NO NEED TO TELL YOU THAT INJURIES INCURRED DURING BATTLE ARE OFTEN SEVERE AS WELL AS EXCRUTIATINGLY PAINFUL.
IT IS ESSENTIAL THAT THESE DEDICATED FIGHTERS FOR OUR CAUSE HAVE A SPEEDY RECOVERY. THEY NEED YOUR ENERGY MORE THAN THE REST OF US DO . . .
YOU'RE NOT SUGGESTING THAT I . . .
IT'S NOT A SUGGESTION OR A REQUEST,
IT'S YOUR DUTY.
FIN

FEASTING THE DEAD

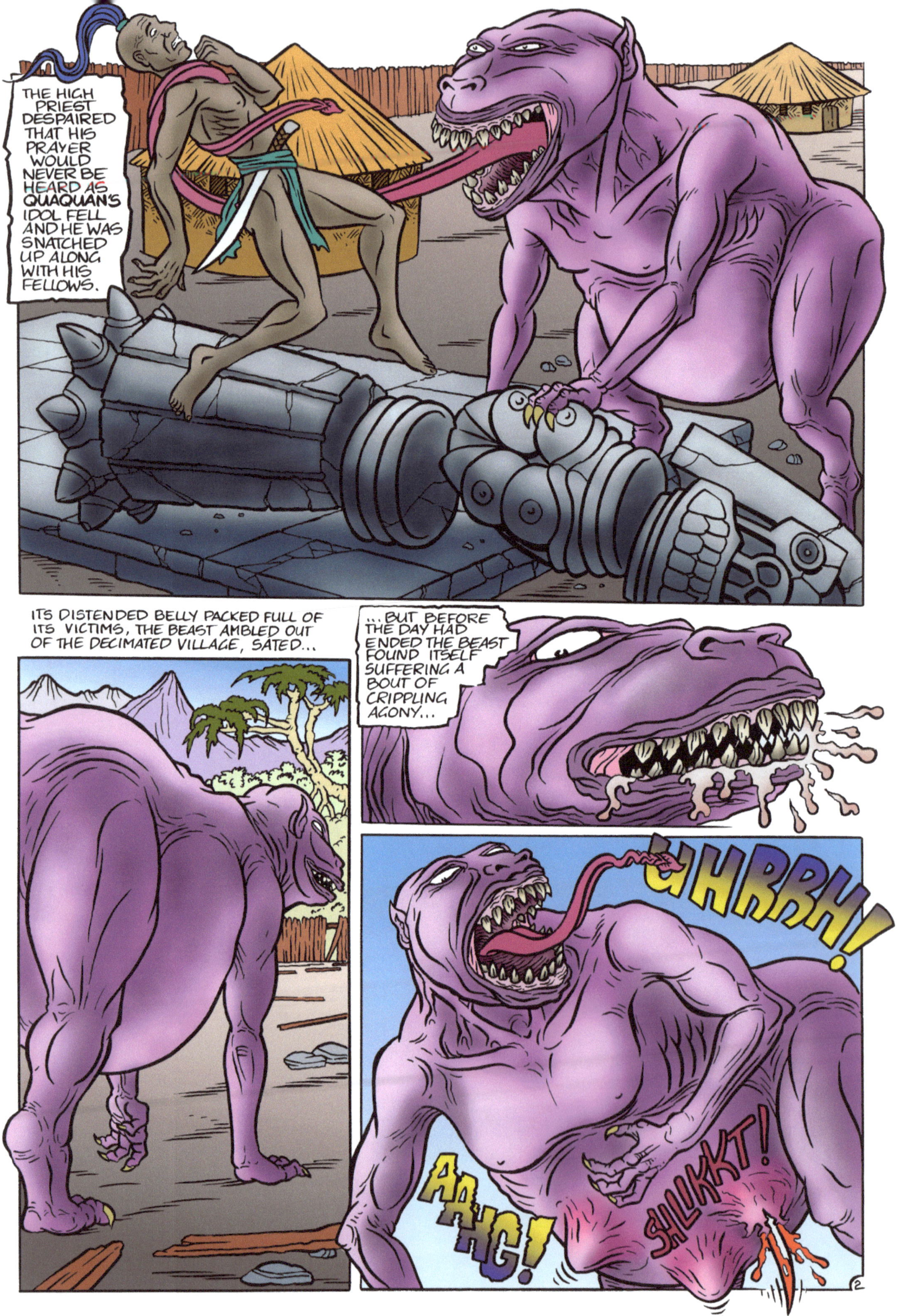

THE HIGH PRIEST DESPAIRED THAT HIS PRAYER WOULD NEVER BE HEARD AS QUAQUAN'S IDOL FELL AND HE WAS SNATCHED UP ALONG WITH HIS FELLOWS.
ITS DISTENDED BELLY PACKED FULL OF ITS VICTIMS, THE BEAST AMBLED OUT OF THE DECIMATED VILLAGE, SATED...
...BUT BEFORE THE DAY HAD ENDED THE BEAST FOUND ITSELF SUFFERING A BOUT OF CRIPPLING AGONY...
UHRRH!
AAHG!
SHLUKKT!

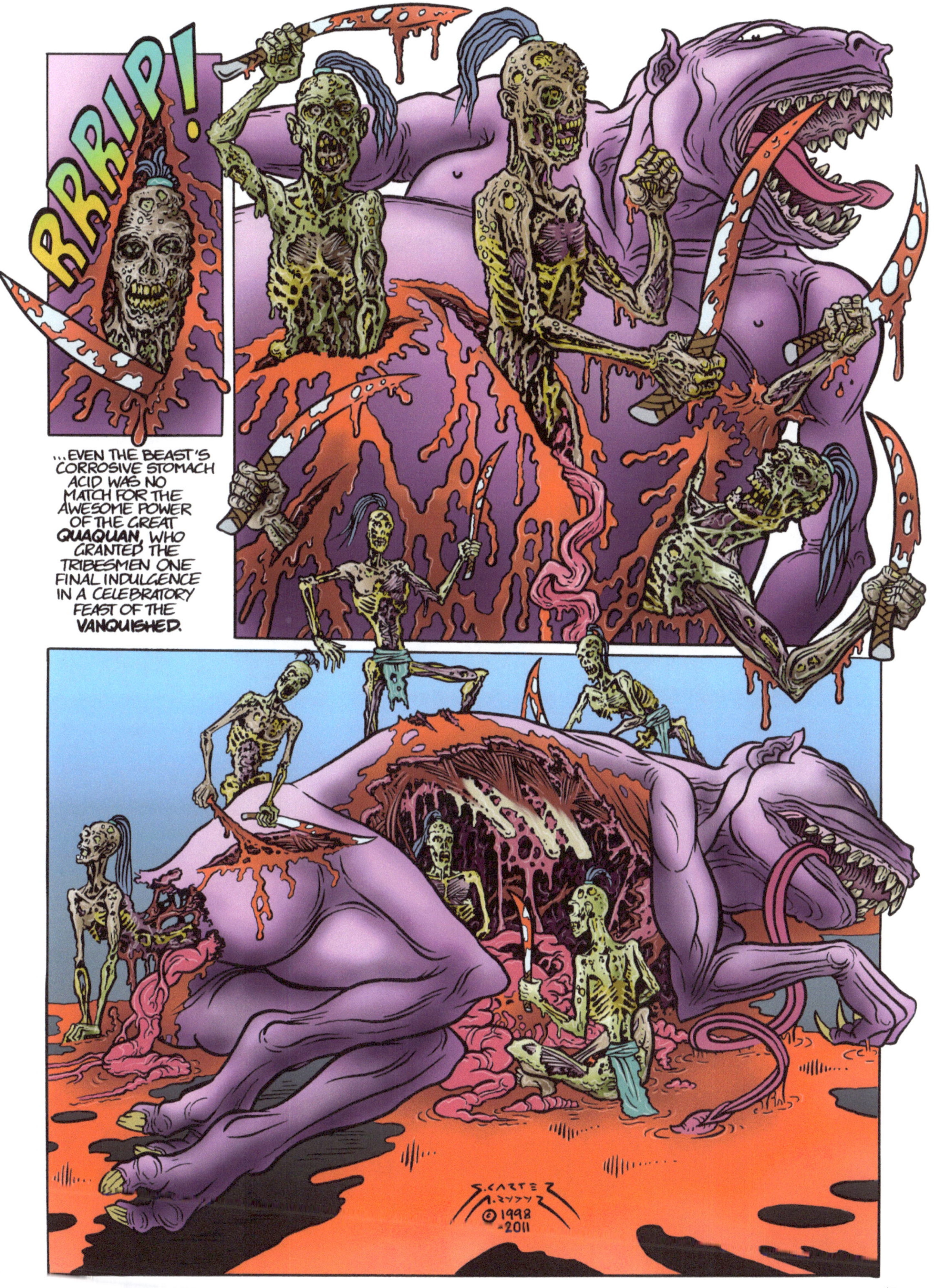

RRRIP!
...EVEN THE BEAST'S CORROSIVE STOMACH ACID WAS NO MATCH FOR THE AWESOME POWER OF THE GREAT QUAQUAN, WHO GRANTED THE TRIBESMEN ONE FINAL INDULGENCE IN A CELEBRATORY FEAST OF THE VANQUISHED.
S. CARTER
© 1998 -2011

DAMNATION

STORY, ART AND CONCEPT © 1997 STEVE CARTER AND ANTOINETTE RYDYR

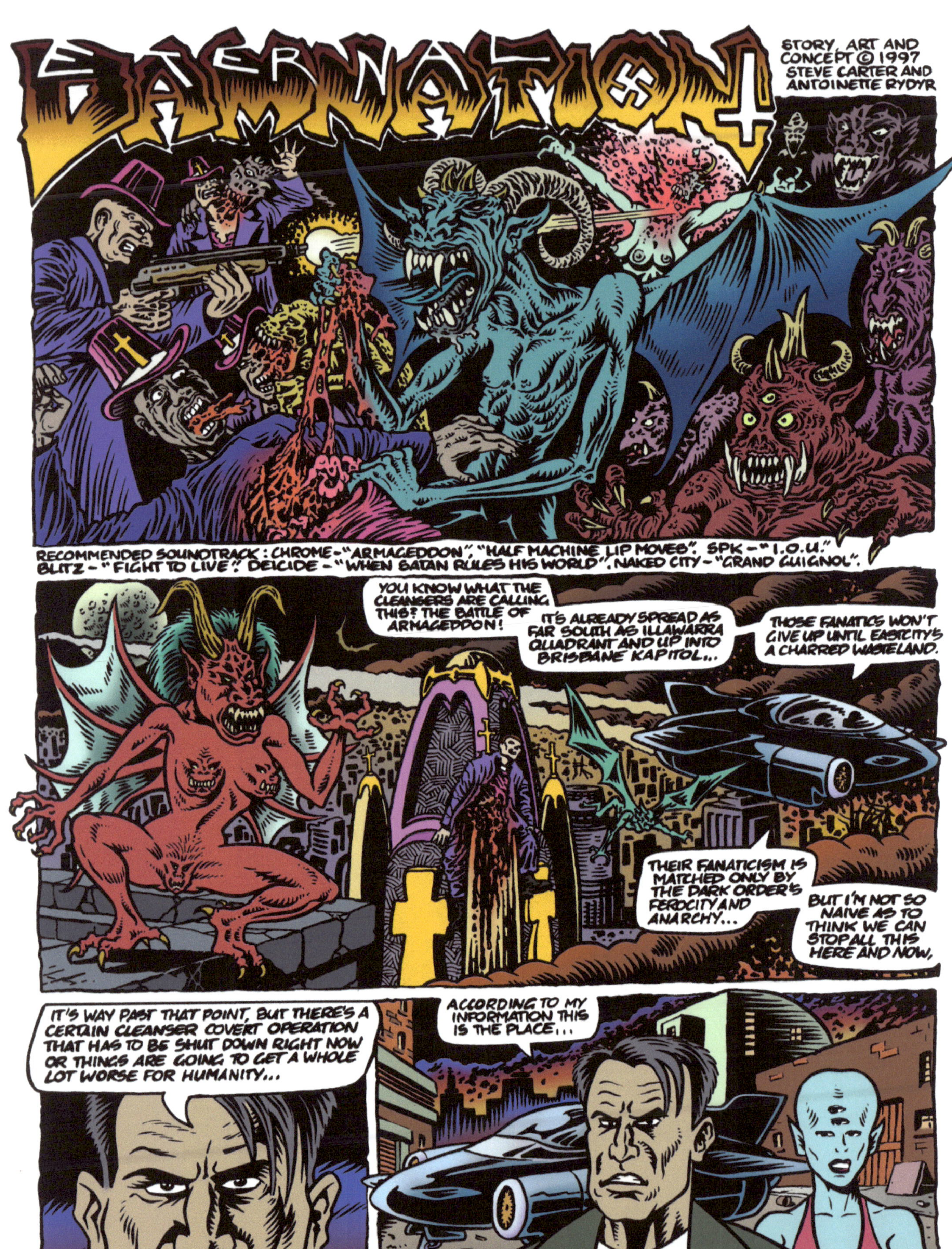

RECOMMENDED SOUNDTRACK: CHROME - "ARMAGEDDON", "HALF MACHINE LIP MOVES", SPK - "I.O.U.". BLITZ - "FIGHT TO LIVE". DEICIDE - "WHEN SATAN RULES HIS WORLD". NAKED CITY - "GRAND GUIGNOL".
YOU KNOW WHAT THE CLEANSERS ARE CALLING THIS? THE BATTLE OF ARMAGEDDON!
IT'S ALREADY SPREAD AS FAR SOUTH AS ILLAWARRA QUADRANT AND UP INTO BRISBANE KAPITOL...
THOSE FANATICS WON'T GIVE UP UNTIL EASTCITY'S A CHARRED WASTELAND.
THEIR FANATICISM IS MATCHED ONLY BY THE DARK ORDER'S FEROCITY AND ANARCHY...
BUT I'M NOT SO NAIVE AS TO THINK WE CAN STOP ALL THIS HERE AND NOW,
IT'S WAY PAST THAT POINT, BUT THERE'S A CERTAIN CLEANSER COVERT OPERATION THAT HAS TO BE SHUT DOWN RIGHT NOW OR THINGS ARE GOING TO GET A WHOLE LOT WORSE FOR HUMANITY...
ACCORDING TO MY INFORMATION THIS IS THE PLACE...

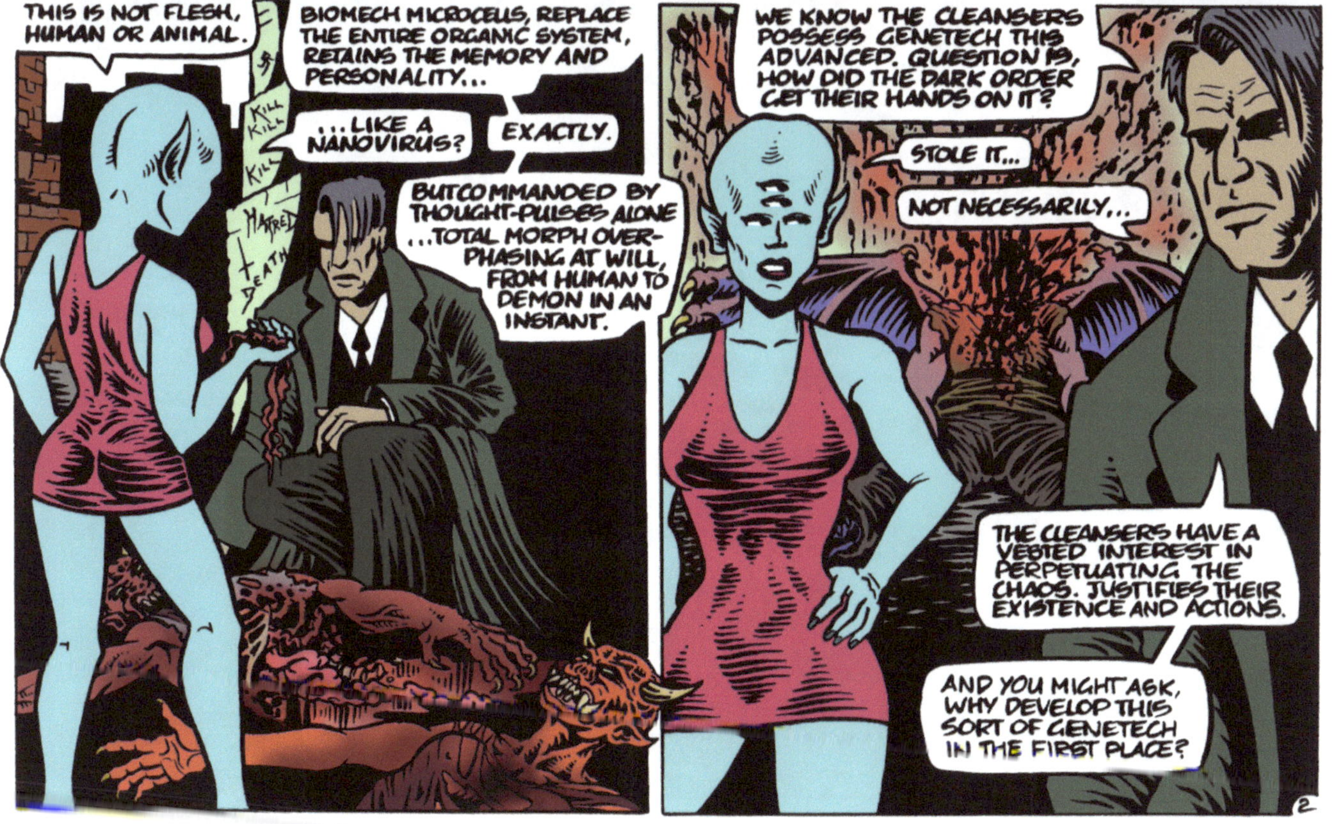

RRGH
Kill the Christian Dog!
DEATH
THIS IS NOT FLESH, HUMAN OR ANIMAL.
BIOMECH MICROCELLS, REPLACE THE ENTIRE ORGANIC SYSTEM, RETAINS THE MEMORY AND PERSONALITY...
...LIKE A NANOVIRUS?
EXACTLY.
BUT COMMANDED BY THOUGHT-PULSES ALONE ...TOTAL MORPH OVER-PHASING AT WILL, FROM HUMAN TO DEMON IN AN INSTANT.
WE KNOW THE CLEANSERS POSSESS GENETECH THIS ADVANCED. QUESTION IS, HOW DID THE DARK ORDER GET THEIR HANDS ON IT?
STOLE IT...
NOT NECESSARILY...
THE CLEANSERS HAVE A VESTED INTEREST IN PERPETUATING THE CHAOS. JUSTIFIES THEIR EXISTENCE AND ACTIONS.
AND YOU MIGHT ASK, WHY DEVELOP THIS SORT OF GENETECH IN THE FIRST PLACE?
We Fight to Live We live to Fight
Kill the Christian
We want PCP not PC

THIS IS IT. WE JUST HAVE TO GET THROUGH THAT...
NO PROBLEM. I CAN INTERFACE WITH THAT SEC-NET IN A MATTER OF SECONDS.

WHAT ARE THEY UP TO?
TIME SLIPPING.
ARE YOU READY TO EMBARK ON YOUR GREAT PILGRIMAGE, BROTHER JOB?
ALWAYS READY TO DO WHAT MUST BE DONE.

HOW DID THESE HEATHENS GET INSIDE THE REDOUBT?
...THAT EGGHEAD! THEY'RE SPECIALLY BRED TO INTERFACE WITH ANY KIND OF SECURITY NETWORK!
CLEANSERS MORPHING INTO DEMONS?! WHAT'S HAPPENING HERE!
ANNIHILATE THEM!

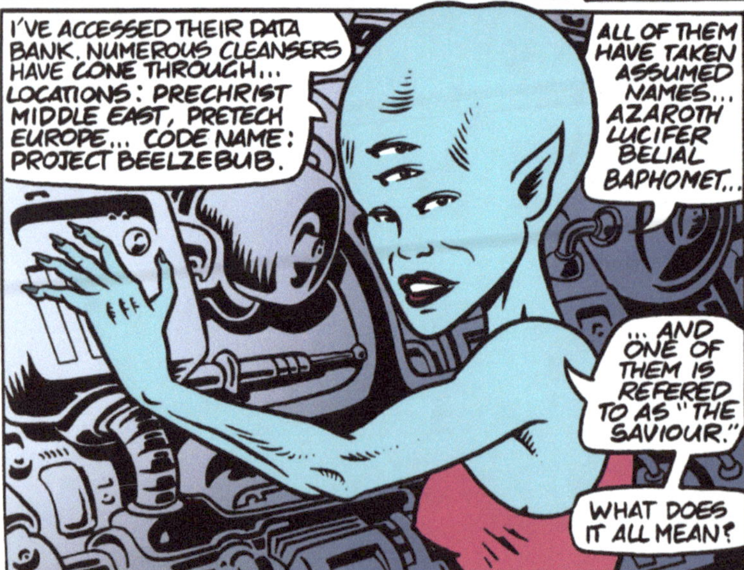

I'VE ACCESSED THEIR DATA BANK, NUMEROUS CLEANSERS HAVE GONE THROUGH... LOCATIONS: PRECHRIST MIDDLE EAST, PRETECH EUROPE... CODE NAME: PROJECT BEELZEBUB.
ALL OF THEM HAVE TAKEN ASSUMED NAMES... AZAROTH LUCIFER BELIAL BAPHOMET...
... AND ONE OF THEM IS REFERED TO AS "THE SAVIOUR."
WHAT DOES IT ALL MEAN?

YOU WANT TO HAVE A LASTING IMPACT ON THE WORLD'S ECONOMY, POLITICS, RELIGION AND CULTURE, YOU CREATE THE DEVIL AND HIS MINIONS, PLANT THEM FIRMLY IN HISTORY. THEN YOU SEND A SAVIOUR WHO COMBATS EVIL AND DIES FOR EVERYONE'S SINS, STIR WITH A MIXTURE OF IGNORANCE FEAR, HYSTERIA, PROPAGANDA...
WE'RE SEVERAL CENTURIES TOO LATE. DAMAGE HAS WELL AND TRULY BEEN DONE.
END.

THE EMiSSARY
STORY:
ANTOINETTE RYDYR
& STEVE CARTER
© 1991- 2012
ART: JASON PAULOS
THE HUNDRED YEAR WAR DEVASTATED MUCH OF PLANET EARTH. THE SURFACE WAS A CHARRED SCAR OF SIZZLING CINDERS. DECAYING MONOLITHS CRUMBLE WHERE ONCE STOOD A BUSTLING METROPOLIS.
MOST ANIMAL LIFE HAS BECOME EXTINCT AND THE REMNANTS OF HUMAN LIFE HAVE SCURRIED FOR SANCTUARY IN CAVES AND DERELICT RUINS.
FEAR SWEPT THE PLANET THAT THE ARMAGEDDON BOMB WOULD OBLITERATE EARTH, EXPLODING IT INTO SPLINTERS OF METEORS AND SPACE DEBRIS.
THE MOST TECHNOLOGICALLY ADVANCED COUNTRIES SENT COLONIES TO NEIGHBOURING PLANETS TO CONTINUE THEIR RACE AND CULTURE AND POSSIBLY THE WAR. PEACE FINALLY SETTLED THE CONFLICT AND EARTH BECAME ONE COHESIVE WORLD NATION.
2514 AD: AMBASSADORS WERE SENT TO ALL OF EARTH'S OFF-WORLD COLONIES TO UNIFY THEM UNDER THE AUSPICE OF HOME-PLANET EARTH...

THE EMISSARY STOOD BEFORE THE REIGNING MONARCHS IN THE ROYAL COURT.
PLEASE YOUR HIGHNESS, I BEG YOU RECONSIDER!
WE HAVE NO INTEREST IN JOINING YOUR "UNION OF COLONISED WORLDS". WE BANISHED THE EVIL THAT CURSED THE EARTH, AND BEGAN ANEW…
"WHEN THIS COLONY WAS SENT FORTH IT WAS TO A BETTER WORLD. WE ARE THE CHOSEN. WE WILL NOT REPEAT THE MISTAKES OF OUR FOREFATHERS."
"IN THE BEGINNING WE STRUGGLED TO SURVIVE BUT WE HAVE TAMED THE LAND AND THERE IS FOOD AND WEALTH ENOUGH FOR ALL."
THERE IS NO GREED, NO HATRED, NO WAR. CAN YOU SAY THE SAME OF YOUR HOME WORLD?

WAR WAS SPAWNED ON EARTH. WE HAVE NO NEED TO RETURN TO ITS VIOLENT WAYS. WE ARE A PEACEFUL PEOPLE.

YOU MAY STAY AS LONG AS YOU PLEASE AND WALK FREELY WITHOUT OBSTRUCTION. AKMIR WILL BE YOUR GUIDE.

THE EMISSARY WAS A VETERAN OF COUNTLESS SUCH OFFICIAL ENGAGEMENTS AND WAS NOT ABOUT TO BE DETERRED.

WHEN YOU HAVE SEEN OUR WORLD YOU MAY REPORT TO YOUR SUPERIORS OF OUR PERFECT SOCIETY SO THAT NO MORE OF YOUR KIND WILL BE SENT HERE TO DISRUPT OUR PEACEFUL HARMONY.

WHAT THE? HEY AKMIR, OLD BUDDY, WHO'S THE GORGEOUS DOLL?

KEEP YOUR DISTANCE EARTHMAN. WE DO NOT EXPRESS LUSTFUL INTENTIONS PUBLICLY. I URGE YOU NOT TO ENTERTAIN LASCIVIOUS THOUGHTS ABOUT THE UNTOUCHED.

'MY KIND' HUH? WELL THAT'S LOVELY, FRIEND AKMIR. YOU MUST HAVE FLUNKED OUT OF CHARM SCHOOL!

ONLY THE MOST BEAUTIFUL GIRLS ARE CHOSEN TO TEND TO THE DEMANDS AND WISHES OF THE MONKS.
THEY WORK IN THE *BENDALA*.
WHAT DO THESE MONKS DO? BESIDES STARING AT THE BEAUTIFUL GAMS THAT ARE ON DISPLAY, THAT IS…?
THOSE INITIATED INTO THE MONKHOOD NEED NEVER DO ANOTHER DAY'S WORK. THEIR EVERY NEED IS TAKEN CARE OF BY *THE UNTOUCHED*.
SOUNDS JUST SWELL!
BE NOT SO FLIPPANT, DANIEL BARLOW. IT IS A *GREAT PRIVILEGE* FOR A MAN TO BE CHOSEN TO BE A MONK. ONLY THOSE WHO HAVE EXCELLED THEMSELVES OR PERFORMED A DEED OF GREAT COURAGE ARE REWARDED THUSLY.

GIVE US YOUR REPORT EMISSARY BARLOW. WHAT HAVE YOU LEARNED ABOUT THEIR ATTITUDES TOWARD US?
I'VE TOURED THE PALACE, THE FIELDS, THE PEASANT HOMES… THE KING IS ADAMANT THAT HE WANTS NO PART OF OUR UNIFICATION PROGRAM.
"BUT I BELIEVE THAT IF I CAN BECOME INVOLVED IN THEIR CULTURE I CAN GAIN THEIR CONFIDENCE AND CONVINCE THEM OF OUR AIMS."
PERHAPS IF YOUR KING AND MEMBERS OF YOUR COURT WERE TO TRAVEL TO EARTH YOU WOULD FIND THAT YOUR FEARS ARE UNFOUNDED.
AS YOU HAVE SEEN, WE ARE A HARMONIOUS SOCIETY. WE ARE SELF-SUFFICIENT. WE HAVE NO NEED TO BECOME INVOLVED IN EARTH'S POLITICS!

DIPLOMACY IS RARELY BLOODLESS HOWEVER...
RIIIPP!!
IT'S A BLOOD REAVER! PROTECT THE QUEEN!
HISSS!!
IT'S A TERRORIST ASSASSINATION PLOT!
EEEK!
HOLD ON, YOUR MAJESTY! I'M COMING!
HISSSS!!
GET IT OFF ME! SOMEBODY HELP!
SO MUCH FOR A 'PEACEFUL SOCIETY' YOUR MAJESTY.
SEEMS NOT ALL YOUR CONSTITUENTS FEEL AS YOU DO!
SCREECH!

I AM GREATLY INDEBTED TO YOU, DANIEL BARLOW. FOR YOUR COURAGE YOU WILL BE BESTOWED OUR GREATEST HONOUR … ENTRY INTO THE BENDALA.
"CEREMONIAL ROBES WILL BE SEWN."
"THE BONDS OF LABOUR WILL BE SMASHED…"
"YOU WILL NEVER NEED TO WORK AGAIN…"
C'MON BABY, I CAN'T TAKE THIS ANY MORE! I'M NOT JUST ANY OLD MONK … YOU'RE A WOMAN. DON'T YOU HAVE DESIRES AS WELL?
NOT YET. IT IS FORBIDDEN. AFTER YOUR INITIATION YOUR EVERY WISH WILL BE MY COMMAND.
SO THE EARTHMAN INGRATIATES HIMSELF INTO OUR HEATHEN CULTURE. NOW I'VE SEEN EVERYTHING. IF I DIDN'T KNOW BETTER I'D SAY YOU SET THAT LITTLE PERFORMANCE UP YOURSELF!
YOU WOUND ME AKMIR, OLD PAL … IF I DIDN'T KNOW BETTER I'D THINK YOU WERE ACTUALLY JEALOUS OF WHAT I'M ABOUT TO RECEIVE!

IN DANIEL BARLOW'S CHAMBERS A VOICE ECHOES …
BARLOW! THIS IS THE THIRD ATTEMPT AT CONTACT. I'M WARNING YOU, BARLOW … YOU WILL FACE DISCIPLINARY ACTION IF YOU'RE FOUND A.W.O.L!
JEALOUS! THAT'S A GOOD ONE, EARTHMAN. JEALOUS! HA HA HA!
"WITHOUT ARMS YOU WILL NO LONGER NEED TO TOIL. YOU WILL BE FREE TO EXPAND YOUR SPIRITUAL CONSCIOUSNESS AND PURSUE INTELLECTUAL ADVANCEMENT…"
"WITHOUT EYES YOU WILL NO LONGER BE DISTRACTED BY THE SURROUNDS OF THE MUNDANE. YOU WILL 'SEE' VISIONS NEVER BEFORE EXPERIENCED
"FOREVER …"

THE ANSWER

SCAZ © 2002-11

SLEEPING BY THE FIRE AGAIN, RAQUELLE?

WHAT DO YOU DREAM ABOUT, I WONDER...

EKAZ ©2002

Jigsaw

by S.C.A.R.
Antoinette Rydyr
& Steve Carter
1991 – 2016

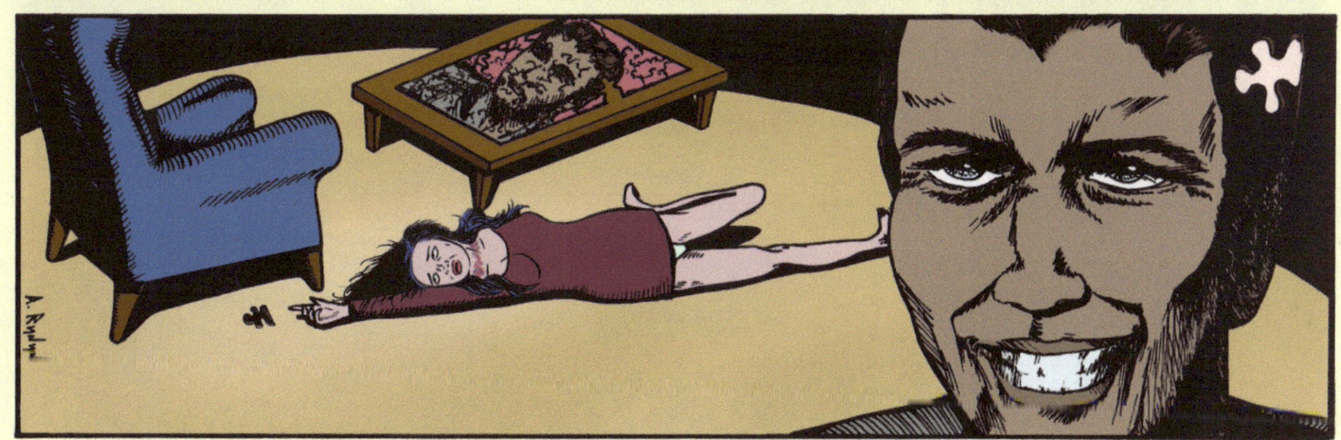

HE CAME BACK

STORY BY STEVE CARTER, 1986
SCRIPT & ART BY FRED ENROHT, 1986
COLOURS & LETTERING BY ANTOINETTE RYDYR, 2016

SMASH

THE CROSSROADS.

"THE CURSE OF THE CROSS-ROADS" I REMEMBER READING ABOUT IT IN THAT GORE MAG.

THAT WOULD EXPLAIN WHY I'M NOT DEAD.
YIP?

AND THESE FANGS ... AND THIS DESIIRE ...
YIPE!

... WHICH I MUST SATISFY.
GURGLE

GURGLE

CREAK

IS THAT YOU VIC?
YEAH
GURGLE

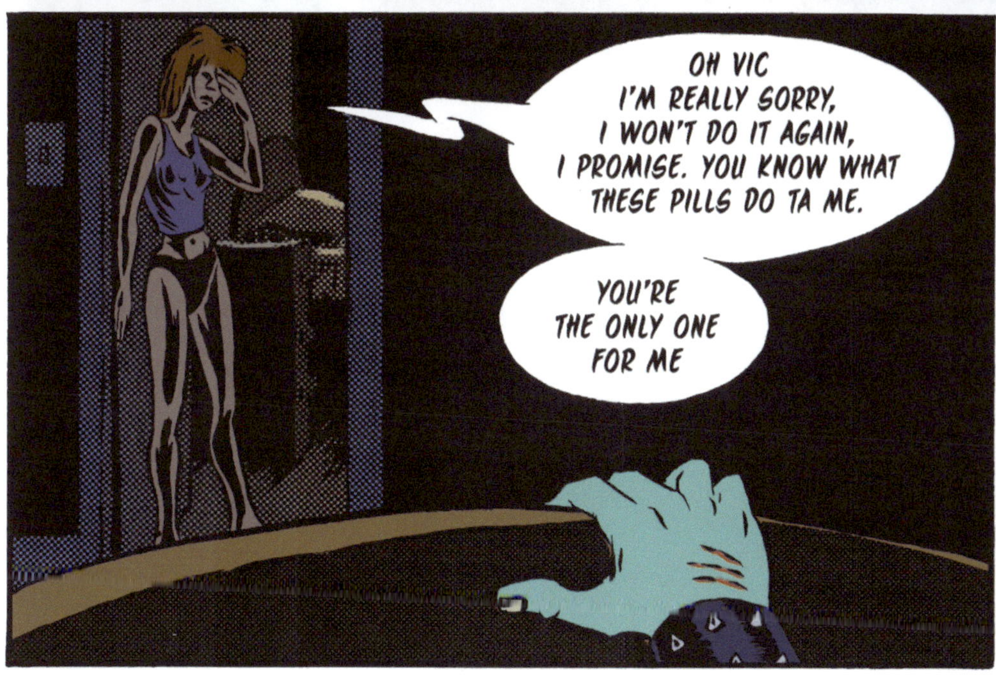
OH VIC
I'M REALLY SORRY,
I WON'T DO IT AGAIN,
I PROMISE. YOU KNOW WHAT
THESE PILLS DO TA ME.
YOU'RE
THE ONLY ONE
FOR ME

CLICK

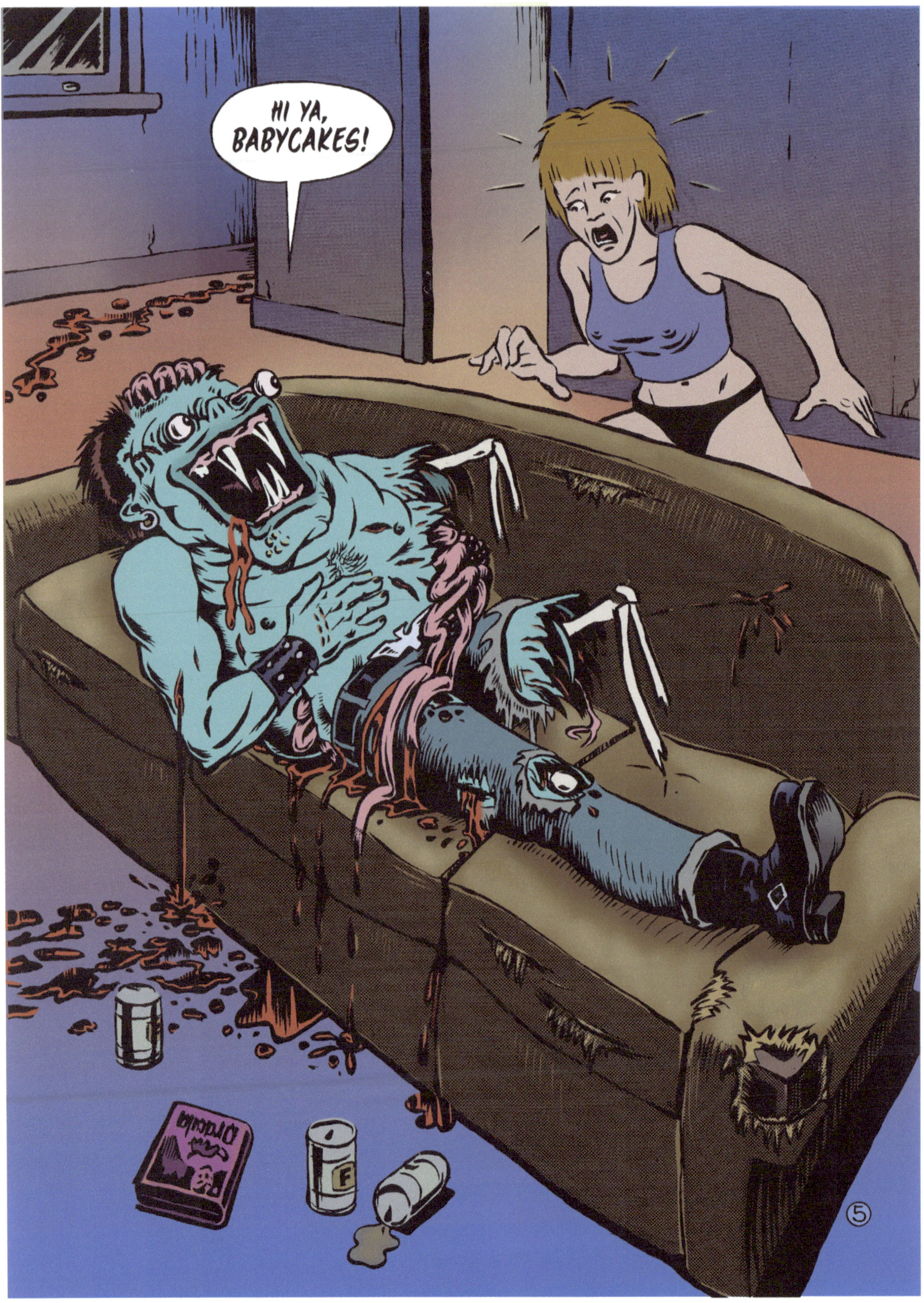

HI YA,
BABYCAKES!

AAH

SLAM

GOTTA THINK A SOMETHIN' FAST! OR THAT THING THAT USED TO BE VIC IS GONNA SUCK ME DRY ... ALL THOSE PILLS I TOOK ... NEED SLEEP BAD.
BASH

IT MIGHT JUST WORK. AT LEAST IT DOES IN THE MOVIES.

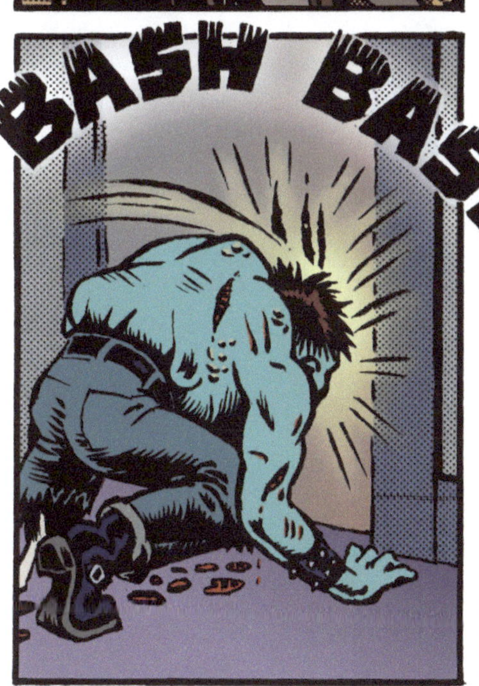

BASH BASH

GURGLE

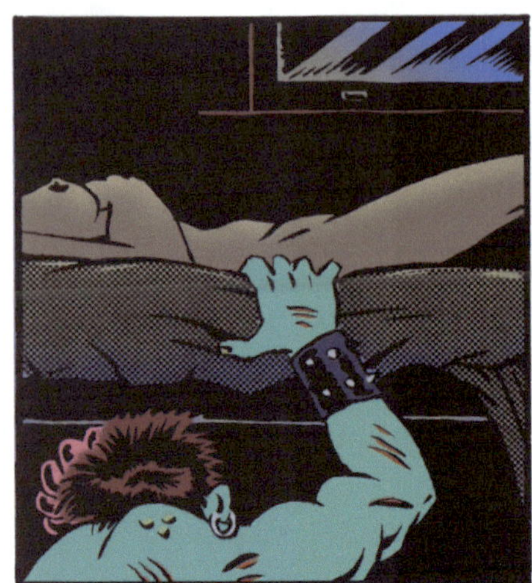

THE BITCH!

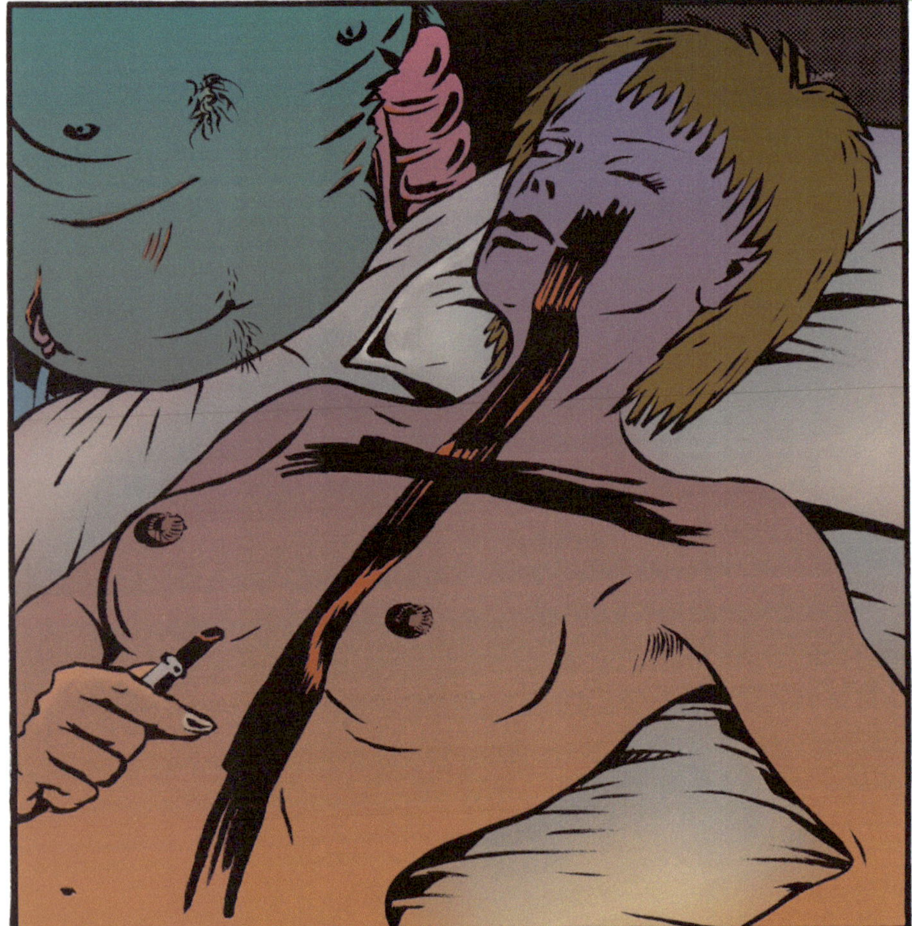

WHAT CAN I DO?

THERE MUST BE SOME WAY AROUND THIS ...

... AND HERE IT IS.

OUR LIPS MEET ... THE FINAL KISS!
SLOP SLURP

SEE YA BABYCAKES. URP
END

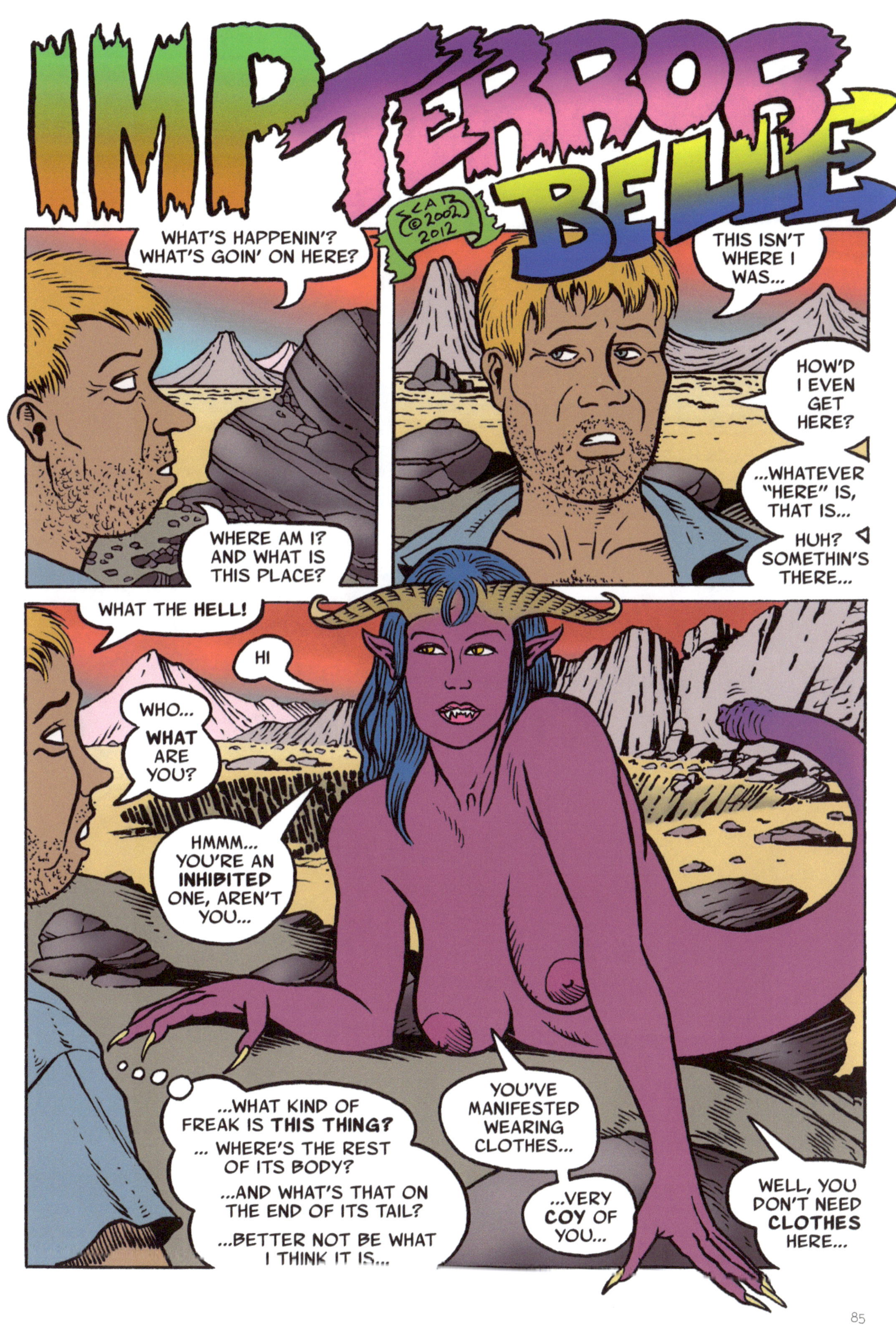

IMP TERROR BELLE
SCAR © 2002 2012
WHAT'S HAPPENIN'? WHAT'S GOIN' ON HERE?
THIS ISN'T WHERE I WAS...
WHERE AM I? AND WHAT IS THIS PLACE?
HOW'D I EVEN GET HERE?
...WHATEVER "HERE" IS, THAT IS...
HUH? SOMETHIN'S THERE...
WHAT THE HELL!
HI
WHO... WHAT ARE YOU?
HMMM... YOU'RE AN INHIBITED ONE, AREN'T YOU...
...WHAT KIND OF FREAK IS THIS THING?
... WHERE'S THE REST OF ITS BODY?
...AND WHAT'S THAT ON THE END OF ITS TAIL?
...BETTER NOT BE WHAT I THINK IT IS...
YOU'VE MANIFESTED WEARING CLOTHES...
...VERY COY OF YOU...
WELL, YOU DON'T NEED CLOTHES HERE...

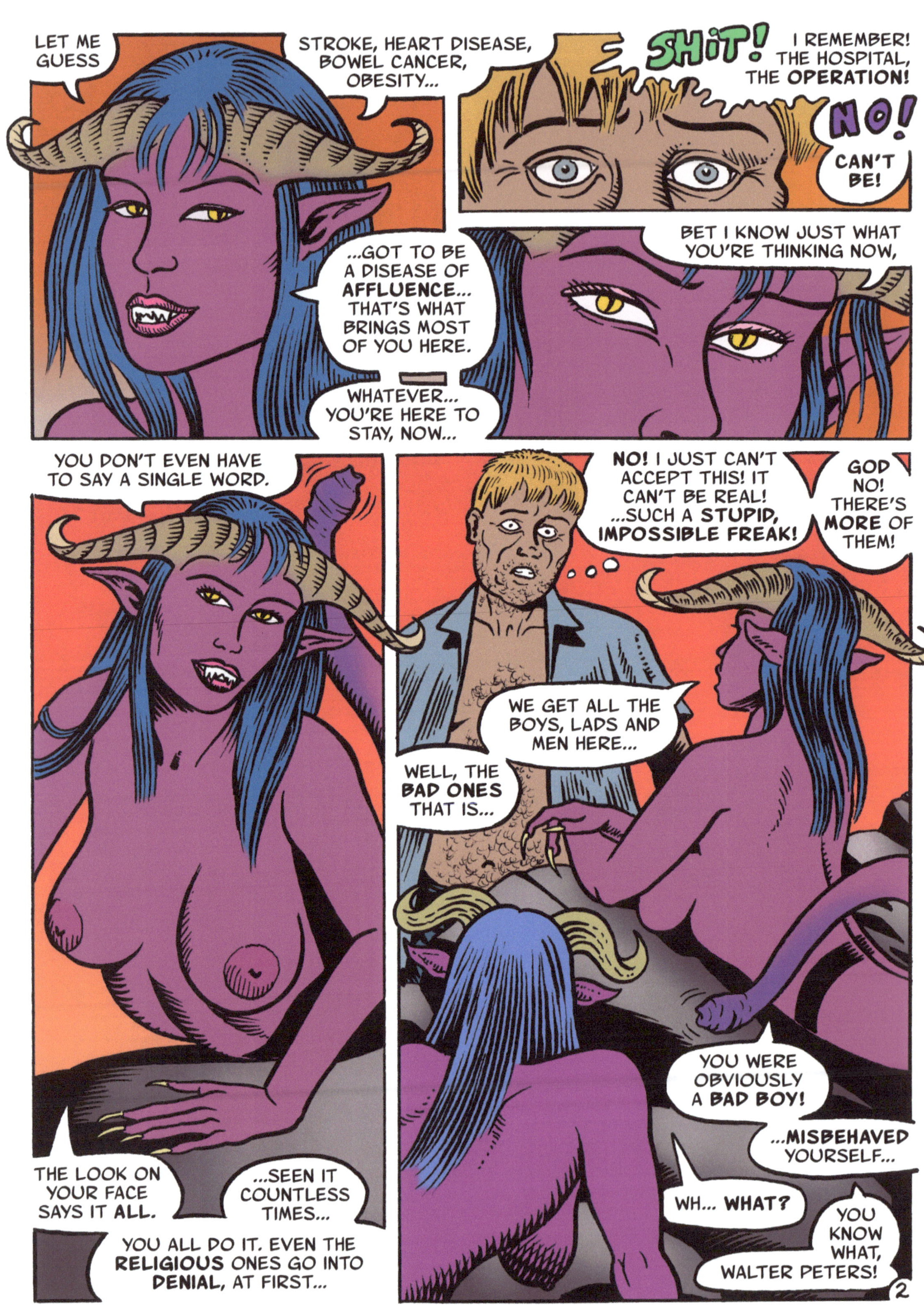

LET ME GUESS
STROKE, HEART DISEASE, BOWEL CANCER, OBESITY...
SHiT!
I REMEMBER! THE HOSPITAL, THE OPERATION!
NO!
CAN'T BE!
...GOT TO BE A DISEASE OF AFFLUENCE... THAT'S WHAT BRINGS MOST OF YOU HERE.
BET I KNOW JUST WHAT YOU'RE THINKING NOW,
WHATEVER... YOU'RE HERE TO STAY, NOW...
YOU DON'T EVEN HAVE TO SAY A SINGLE WORD.
NO! I JUST CAN'T ACCEPT THIS! IT CAN'T BE REAL! ...SUCH A STUPID, IMPOSSIBLE FREAK!
GOD NO! THERE'S MORE OF THEM!
WE GET ALL THE BOYS, LADS AND MEN HERE...
WELL, THE BAD ONES THAT IS...
YOU WERE OBVIOUSLY A BAD BOY!
...MISBEHAVED YOURSELF...
WH... WHAT?
YOU KNOW WHAT, WALTER PETERS!
THE LOOK ON YOUR FACE SAYS IT ALL.
...SEEN IT COUNTLESS TIMES...
YOU ALL DO IT. EVEN THE RELIGIOUS ONES GO INTO DENIAL, AT FIRST...
2

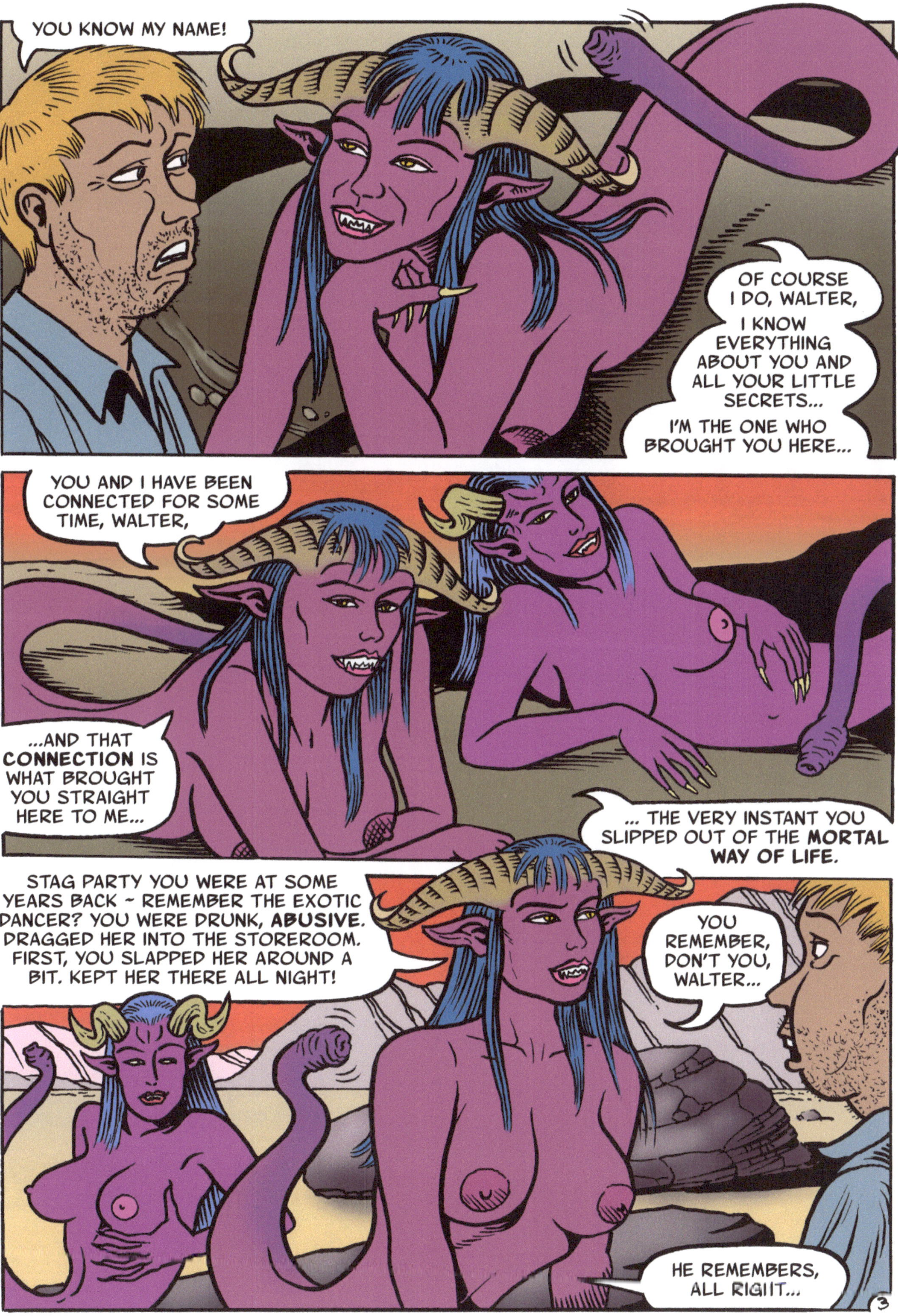

YOU KNOW MY NAME!
OF COURSE I DO, WALTER, I KNOW EVERYTHING ABOUT YOU AND ALL YOUR LITTLE SECRETS...
I'M THE ONE WHO BROUGHT YOU HERE...
YOU AND I HAVE BEEN CONNECTED FOR SOME TIME, WALTER,
...AND THAT CONNECTION IS WHAT BROUGHT YOU STRAIGHT HERE TO ME...
... THE VERY INSTANT YOU SLIPPED OUT OF THE MORTAL WAY OF LIFE.
STAG PARTY YOU WERE AT SOME YEARS BACK ~ REMEMBER THE EXOTIC DANCER? YOU WERE DRUNK, ABUSIVE. DRAGGED HER INTO THE STOREROOM. FIRST, YOU SLAPPED HER AROUND A BIT. KEPT HER THERE ALL NIGHT!
YOU REMEMBER, DON'T YOU, WALTER...
HE REMEMBERS, ALL RIGIIT...

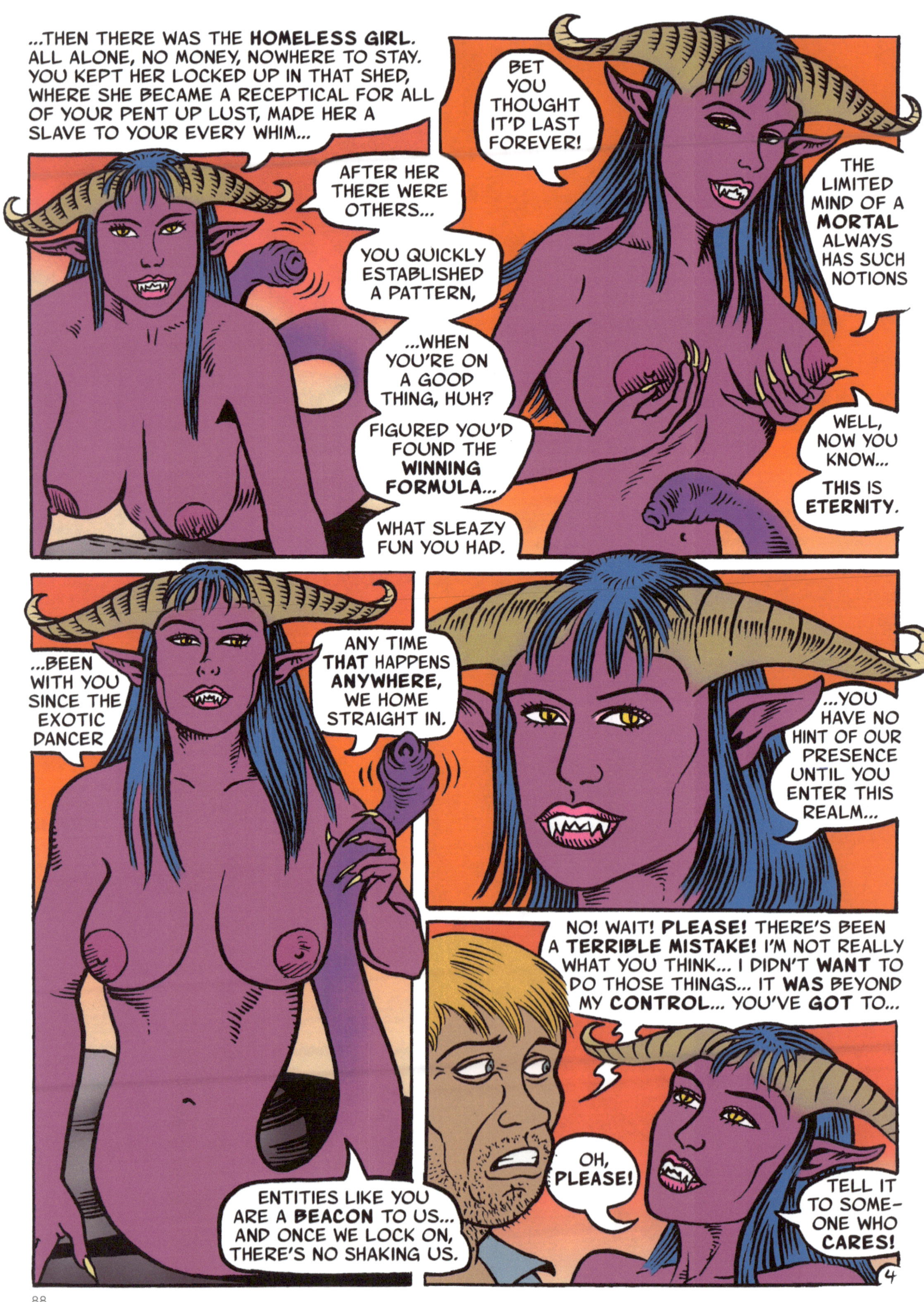

...THEN THERE WAS THE HOMELESS GIRL. ALL ALONE, NO MONEY, NOWHERE TO STAY. YOU KEPT HER LOCKED UP IN THAT SHED, WHERE SHE BECAME A RECEPTICAL FOR ALL OF YOUR PENT UP LUST, MADE HER A SLAVE TO YOUR EVERY WHIM...
BET YOU THOUGHT IT'D LAST FOREVER!
THE LIMITED MIND OF A MORTAL ALWAYS HAS SUCH NOTIONS
AFTER HER THERE WERE OTHERS...
YOU QUICKLY ESTABLISHED A PATTERN,
...WHEN YOU'RE ON A GOOD THING, HUH?
FIGURED YOU'D FOUND THE WINNING FORMULA...
WHAT SLEAZY FUN YOU HAD.
WELL, NOW YOU KNOW...
THIS IS ETERNITY.
...BEEN WITH YOU SINCE THE EXOTIC DANCER
ANY TIME THAT HAPPENS ANYWHERE, WE HOME STRAIGHT IN.
...YOU HAVE NO HINT OF OUR PRESENCE UNTIL YOU ENTER THIS REALM...
NO! WAIT! PLEASE! THERE'S BEEN A TERRIBLE MISTAKE! I'M NOT REALLY WHAT YOU THINK... I DIDN'T WANT TO DO THOSE THINGS... IT WAS BEYOND MY CONTROL... YOU'VE GOT TO...
ENTITIES LIKE YOU ARE A BEACON TO US... AND ONCE WE LOCK ON, THERE'S NO SHAKING US.
OH, PLEASE!
TELL IT TO SOME-ONE WHO CARES!
4

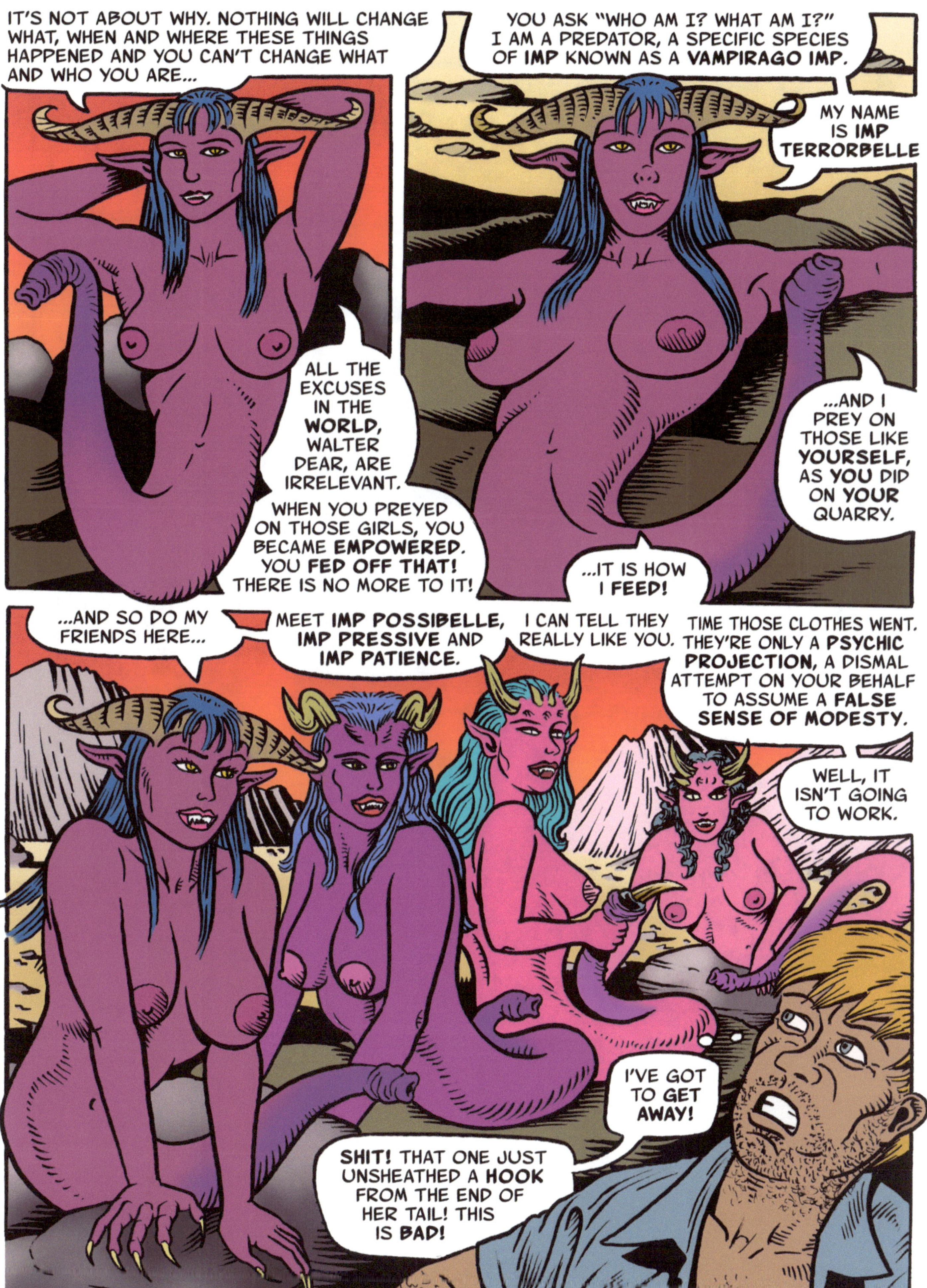

IT'S NOT ABOUT WHY. NOTHING WILL CHANGE WHAT, WHEN AND WHERE THESE THINGS HAPPENED AND YOU CAN'T CHANGE WHAT AND WHO YOU ARE...
YOU ASK "WHO AM I? WHAT AM I?" I AM A PREDATOR, A SPECIFIC SPECIES OF IMP KNOWN AS A VAMPIRAGO IMP.
MY NAME IS IMP TERRORBELLE
ALL THE EXCUSES IN THE WORLD, WALTER DEAR, ARE IRRELEVANT.
WHEN YOU PREYED ON THOSE GIRLS, YOU BECAME EMPOWERED. YOU FED OFF THAT! THERE IS NO MORE TO IT!
...AND I PREY ON THOSE LIKE YOURSELF, AS YOU DID ON YOUR QUARRY.
...IT IS HOW I FEED!
...AND SO DO MY FRIENDS HERE...
MEET IMP POSSIBELLE, IMP PRESSIVE AND IMP PATIENCE.
I CAN TELL THEY REALLY LIKE YOU.
TIME THOSE CLOTHES WENT. THEY'RE ONLY A PSYCHIC PROJECTION, A DISMAL ATTEMPT ON YOUR BEHALF TO ASSUME A FALSE SENSE OF MODESTY.
WELL, IT ISN'T GOING TO WORK.
SHIT! THAT ONE JUST UNSHEATHED A HOOK FROM THE END OF HER TAIL! THIS IS BAD!
I'VE GOT TO GET AWAY!

YOU CAN'T ESCAPE US, WALTER.
NOW, WE CAN EITHER BLINK THOSE CLOTHES AWAY,
...OR RIP THEM OFF YOU! THAT'D BE MORE FUN!
GET OFF ME, YOU FREAK!

THIS WORLD IS JUST AS REAL AS THE ONE YOU'VE JUST DEPARTED, AND SO IS EVERY SENSATION THAT YOU FEEL.
BUT WE'RE NOT GOING TO KILL YOU. WE CAN'T. YOU CAN ONLY DIE ONCE.
...YOU'VE ALREADY DONE THAT...
DON'T TAKE IT SO BADLY, WALTER. YOU'LL LIVE. ME THINKS YOU PROTESTETH TOO MUCH.
AAEEiiGH!

NEVER THOUGHT I'D SEE THE LIGHT OF DAY AGAIN, LET ALONE ACTUALLY BE ABLE TO WALK AGAIN.
...REALLY DIDN'T EXPECT TO MAKE IT,
BUT HERE I AM, FOUR MONTHS LATER AND WELL ON THE WAY TO A FULL RECOVERY...

...BUT THAT HIDEOUS DREAM STILL HAUNTS ME! ...SO VIVID, SO TWISTED!
IT'S COMPLETELY UNFATHOMABLE!
SURELY EVEN THE DEEPEST RECESSES OF MY SUBCONSCIOUS MIND COULDN'T POSSIBLY CREAT SUCH A WEIRD, DERANGED SCENARIO?
MY COUNSELLOR INSISTS IT WAS THE PRODUCT OF EXTREME STRESS, UNLEASHING HIDDEN FEARS WHICH CAN "OFTEN MANIFEST IN BIZARRE WAYS..."

...AND THE SHRINK ASSURES ME I'M NOT INSANE AND THAT IN DUE TIME MY LIFE WILL AGAIN BE NORMAL...

HMMM, HOW ODD! DON'T REMEMBER THIS AREA...
WELL, IT'S BEEN A WHILE SINCE I'VE BEEN HERE.
PERHAPS I'VE NEVER COME ALONG THIS PARTICULAR PATHWAY BEFORE...
VERY DRY, ROCKY... NO HERBAGE...

7

HI, WALTER. I'M STILL HERE, AND SO ARE YOU.
NO, YOU DIDN'T SURVIVE THAT OPERATION. ...JUST BEEN MESSIN' WITH YOUR MIND... ...BECAUSE I CAN.
AD INFINITUM...

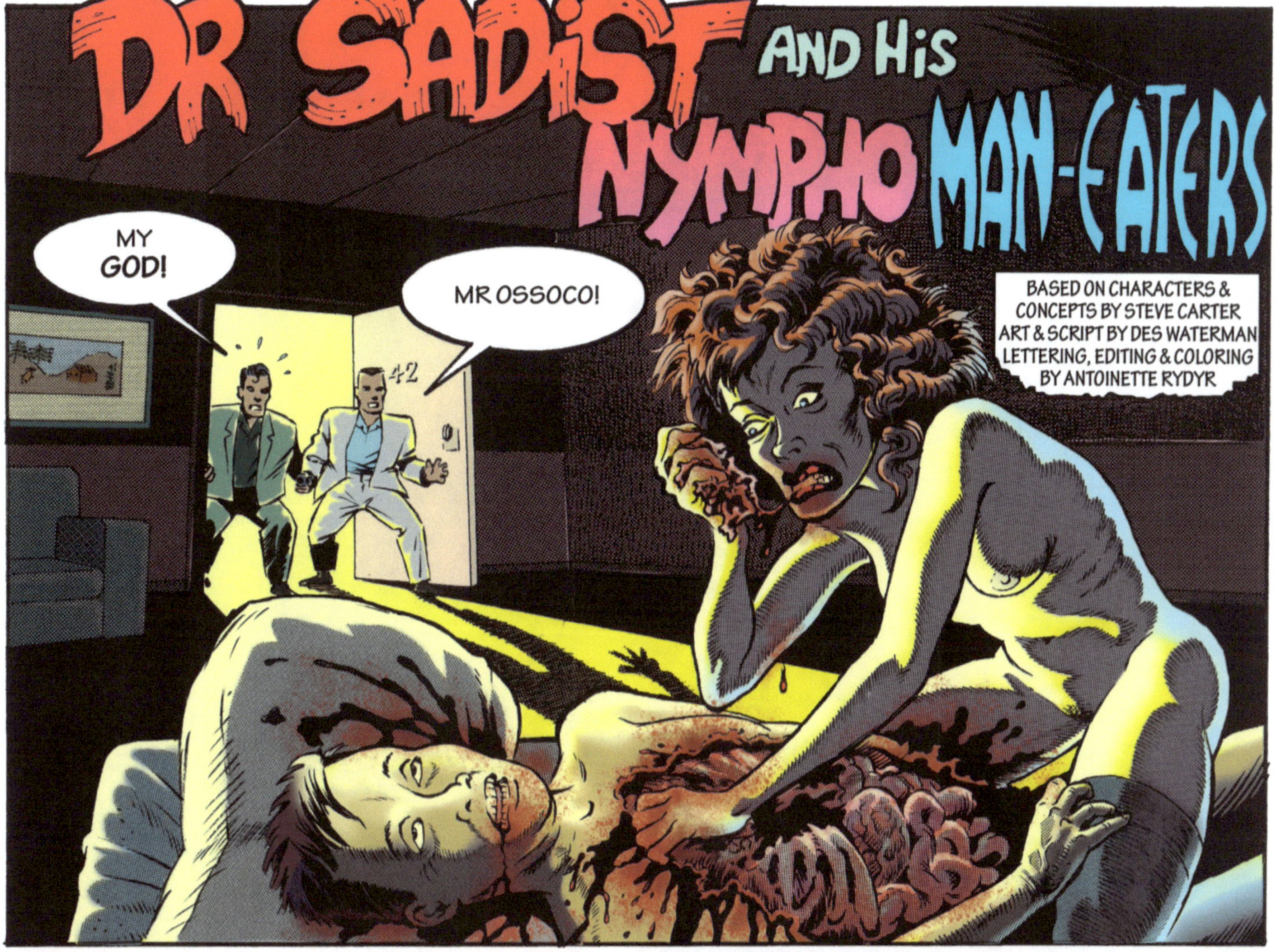

DR SADIST AND HIS NYMPHO MAN-EATERS

BASED ON CHARACTERS &
CONCEPTS BY STEVE CARTER
ART & SCRIPT BY DES WATERMAN
LETTERING, EDITING & COLORING
BY ANTOINETTE RYDYR

YOU GO AND CALL THE BOSS. I'LL CLEAN UP IN HERE...
UH HUH!

WHAT! AGAIN? THIS IS GOING TOO FAR!
I GOT A REPUTATION TO PROTECT!

YOU GET OUTTA HERE. I GOT BUSINESS TO DO!
LUCILLE! TELL YA BROTHER I WANNA SPEAK TO HIM!
I DON'T CARE WHAT HE'S DOING! PUT HIM ON!

IT'S LOZARIO. HE SOUNDS ANGRY. HE'S THREATENING TO PULL THE PLUG ON THIS WHOLE OPERATION.
YOU BETTER SPEAK TO HIM...
WAH!
OKAY, OKAY! I'LL TALK TO HIM...

NOW LISTEN HERE, DOC! ANOTHER ONE OF YOUR LITTLE LOVE DOLLS WENT NUTSO ON A CLIENT OF MINE.
HE'S DEAD, SHE'S DEAD AND I'LL BE DEAD, TOO, IF I CAN'T MAKE IT LOOK LIKE AN ACCIDENT!
WHAT IN THE NAME OF FUCK IS GOING ON?

I'VE BEEN ENCOUNTERING THIS PROBLEM. IT SEEMS THAT AFTER THE SEX CENTRE OF THE BRAIN HAS BEEN STIMULATED, A PRIMAL URGE FOR FOOD MANIFESTS,
RESULTING IN...

I'VE SEEN THE RESULTS DOC. THEY EAT THE JOHNS! LISTEN! CLOSE SHOP!
I'M FLYING OVER PERSONALLY TO INSPECT THE OPERATION!

NEXT DAY...
FINALLY GET TA MEET THAT CRAZY DOCTOR, HUH BOSS?
I HEARD HE'S BADLY SCARRED OR SUMTHING...
SO THEY SAY!

I GUESS WE HEAD UP THAT TRAIL, IF I'M READING THIS MAP RIGHT.
PLACE IS A FUCKIN' JUNGLE.

CATCH UP WID YA, GOTTA TAKE A LEAK!
WE'LL WALK SLOW...

HUH!
SHIT BABY! YOU SCARED ME.

WELL DON'T JUST STAND THERE, BABY!
DO SUMTHIN'!

BLAM
BLAM
THAT'S BUD! QUICK, HE'S IN TROUBLE!

I CAN'T BELIEVE IT.... SHE BIT ME DICK OFF!

LOOK OUT! WE'RE SURROUNDED!
WATCH OUT, SISTER! THIS COCK BITES BACK!

BLAM
SPLUTT

C'MON BUD! WE GOTTA MOVE IT!
OHHHH!

BLAT BLAT

PUDAPUDAPUDA
HELL! I LOST MY REASON TO LIVE! I'M STAYIN' PUT!

POOR GUY!
BLAM
LOOK!

OPEN UP, DOC! FER CHRIST'S SAKE!
PUDA PUDA PUDA

THE HUGE DOOR SLIDES OPEN JUST IN TIME...
CRAZY FUCKS!
THAT WAS TOO CLOSE!

THEY BARELY HAVE TIME TO CATCH THEIR BREATH WHEN...
MY GOD! BUT YOU'RE ONE FUCKED UP UGLY MOTHER!
JEEEZ - USS!

WE'LL GENTLEMEN, I'M SURPRISED YOU GOT THIS FAR. I TAKE IT YOU'VE ALREADY...
...MET SOME OF MY REJECTS!
...DO COME IN!

THAT NIGHT OVER DINNER THE DOCTOR ATTEMPTS TO EXPLAIN.
SO YOU SEE, THOSE WERE THE FIRST ONES.
ABSOLUTE FAILURES!
BUT I SOON REALISED MY MISTAKE!

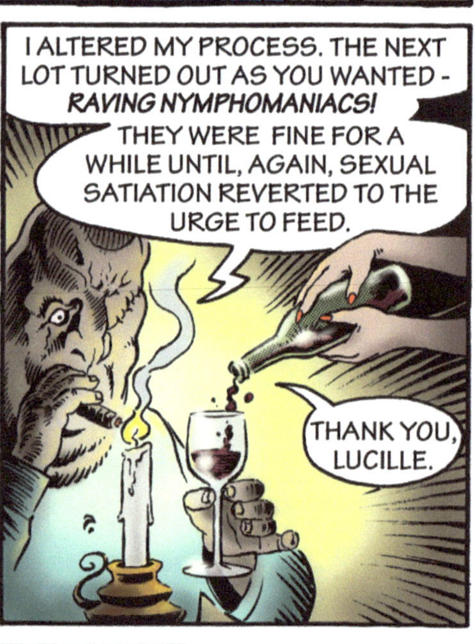

I ALTERED MY PROCESS. THE NEXT LOT TURNED OUT AS YOU WANTED - RAVING NYMPHOMANIACS!
THEY WERE FINE FOR A WHILE UNTIL, AGAIN, SEXUAL SATIATION REVERTED TO THE URGE TO FEED.
THANK YOU, LUCILLE.

AFTER THAT I FURTHER REFINED MY TECHNIQUE. AND I WAS ABLE TO PROLONG THE PERIOD OF NYMPHOMANIA.
FINALLY, I FELT I HAD SUCCEEDED. I SENT THOSE GIRLS TO YOU IN GOOD FAITH.

BUT AS YOU TELL ME, TWO OF THEM DID REVERT AND I ASSUME THAT THE OTHER THREE WILL TOO... ...EVENTUALLY!
NOW, MY FRIENDS. I GUESS... .

YOU'RE WONDERING WHY... YOU'VE BEEN STRAPPED TO THOSE CHAIRS!
YOU SON OF A BITCH!

OBVIOUSLY, MY RESEARCH MUST CONTINUE! I'VE COME THIS FAR, I CAN'T STOP NOW.
MY BROTHER IS A BRILLIANT MAN.
WE STILL HAVE SOME GIRLS LEFT.
MY BROTHER FEELS HE CAN SUCCEED THIS TIME.
BUT WE CAN LEAVE NOTHING TO CHANCE.
THE WAITING PERIOD WILL JUST HAVE TO BE EXTENDED, THAT'S ALL.
NO!
NO MORE MONEY! NO MORE RESEARCH!

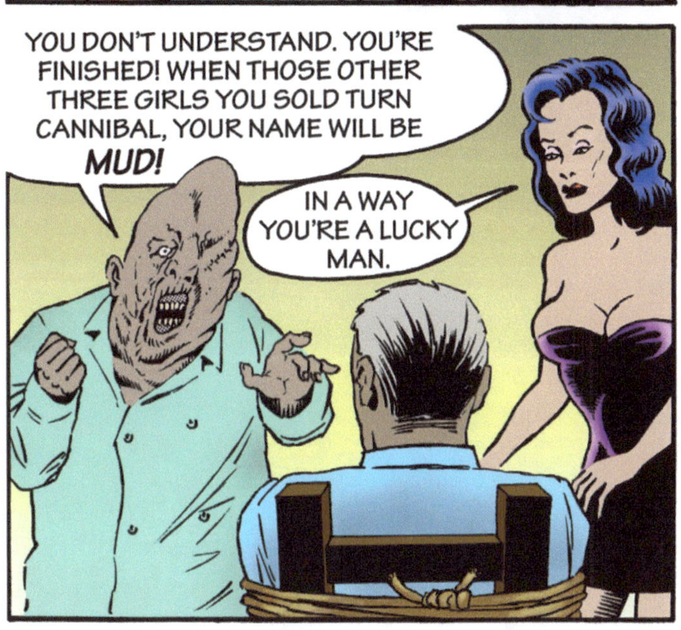

YOU DON'T UNDERSTAND. YOU'RE FINISHED! WHEN THOSE OTHER THREE GIRLS YOU SOLD TURN CANNIBAL, YOUR NAME WILL BE MUD!
IN A WAY YOU'RE A LUCKY MAN.

YES! NO-ONE KNOWS WHERE TO FIND YOU. AND I DON'T NEED YOUR MONEY. WHEN I SUCCEED I'LL HAVE PLENTY OF THAT!
BUT WE DO NEED YOU!

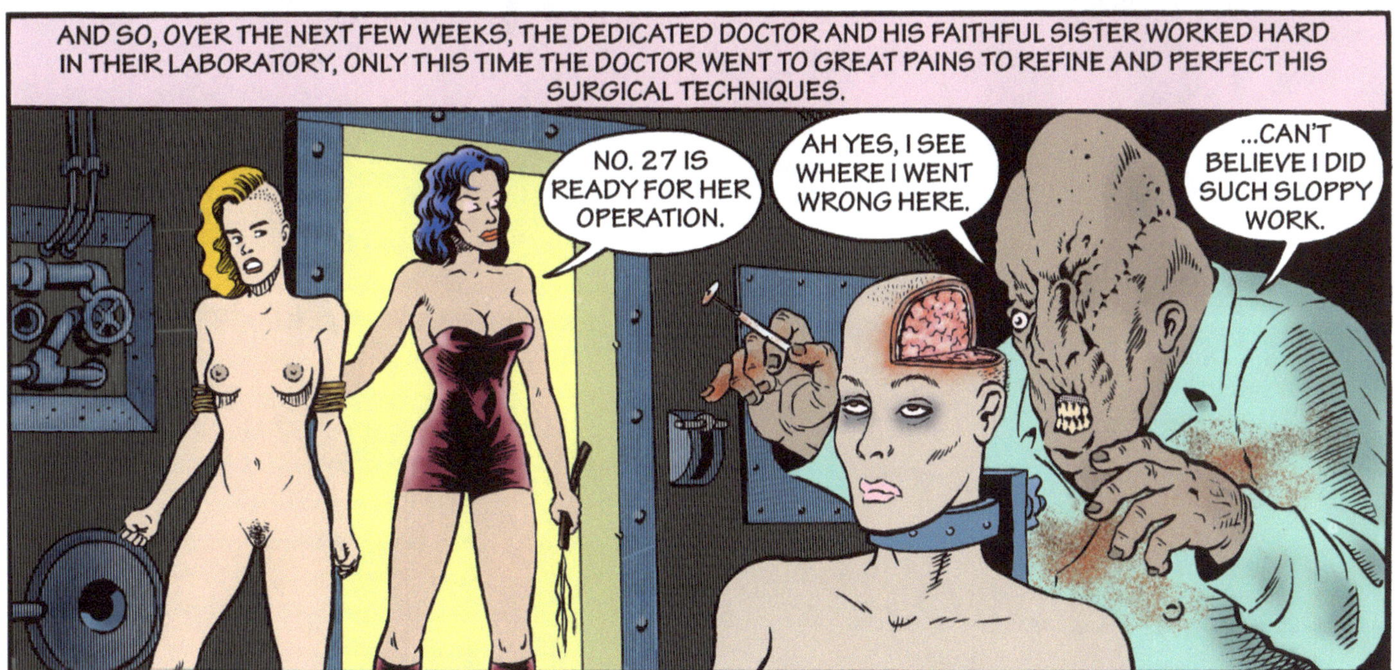

AND SO, OVER THE NEXT FEW WEEKS, THE DEDICATED DOCTOR AND HIS FAITHFUL SISTER WORKED HARD IN THEIR LABORATORY, ONLY THIS TIME THE DOCTOR WENT TO GREAT PAINS TO REFINE AND PERFECT HIS SURGICAL TECHNIQUES.
NO. 27 IS READY FOR HER OPERATION.
AH YES, I SEE WHERE I WENT WRONG HERE,
...CAN'T BELIEVE I DID SUCH SLOPPY WORK.

I'LL GO CHECK ON OUR FRIENDS.
BE QUIET!
NOOO NOOOO!

LUCILLE STRIDES DOWN THE CELL LINED CORRIDOR...
CLICK CLOP
CLICK

OH DEAR, REALLY...
YOU MUSTN'T CRY LIKE THAT...

MY BROTHER IS SURE TO GET IT RIGHT THIS TIME!
YOU'LL SEE!
END.

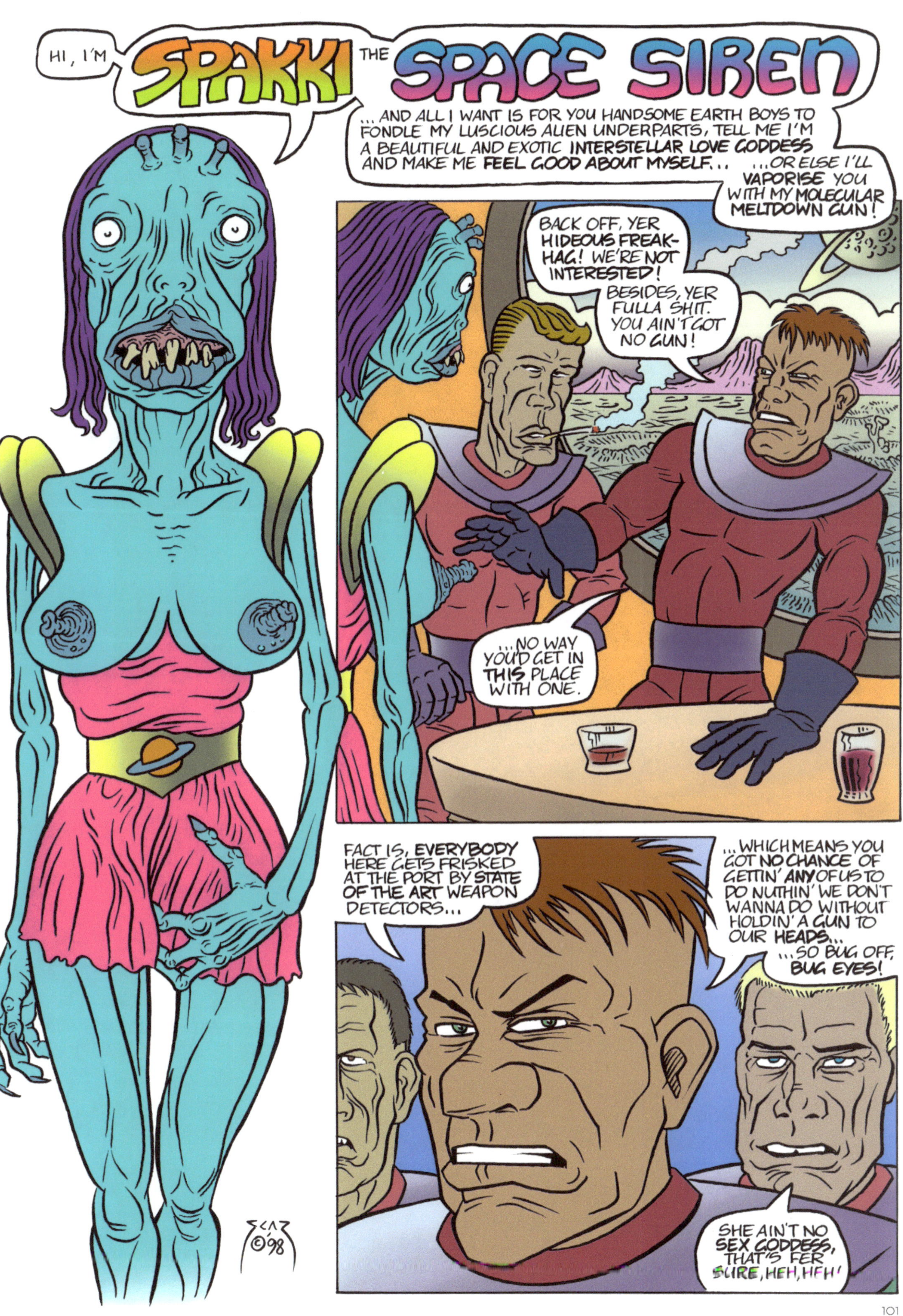

HI, I'M SPAKKI THE SPACE SIREN
...AND ALL I WANT IS FOR YOU HANDSOME EARTH BOYS TO FONDLE MY LUSCIOUS ALIEN UNDERPARTS, TELL ME I'M A BEAUTIFUL AND EXOTIC INTERSTELLAR LOVE GODDESS AND MAKE ME FEEL GOOD ABOUT MYSELF...
...OR ELSE I'LL VAPORISE YOU WITH MY MOLECULAR MELTDOWN GUN!
BACK OFF, YER HIDEOUS FREAK-HAG! WE'RE NOT INTERESTED!
BESIDES, YER FULLA SHIT. YOU AIN'T GOT NO GUN!
...NO WAY YOU'D GET IN THIS PLACE WITH ONE.
FACT IS, EVERYBODY HERE GETS FRISKED AT THE PORT BY STATE OF THE ART WEAPON DETECTORS...
...WHICH MEANS YOU GOT NO CHANCE OF GETTIN' ANY OF US TO DO NUTHIN' WE DON'T WANNA DO WITHOUT HOLDIN' A GUN TO OUR HEADS...
...SO BUG OFF, BUG EYES!
SHE AIN'T NO SEX GODDESS, THAT'S FER SURE, HEH, HEH!
SCAR ©'98

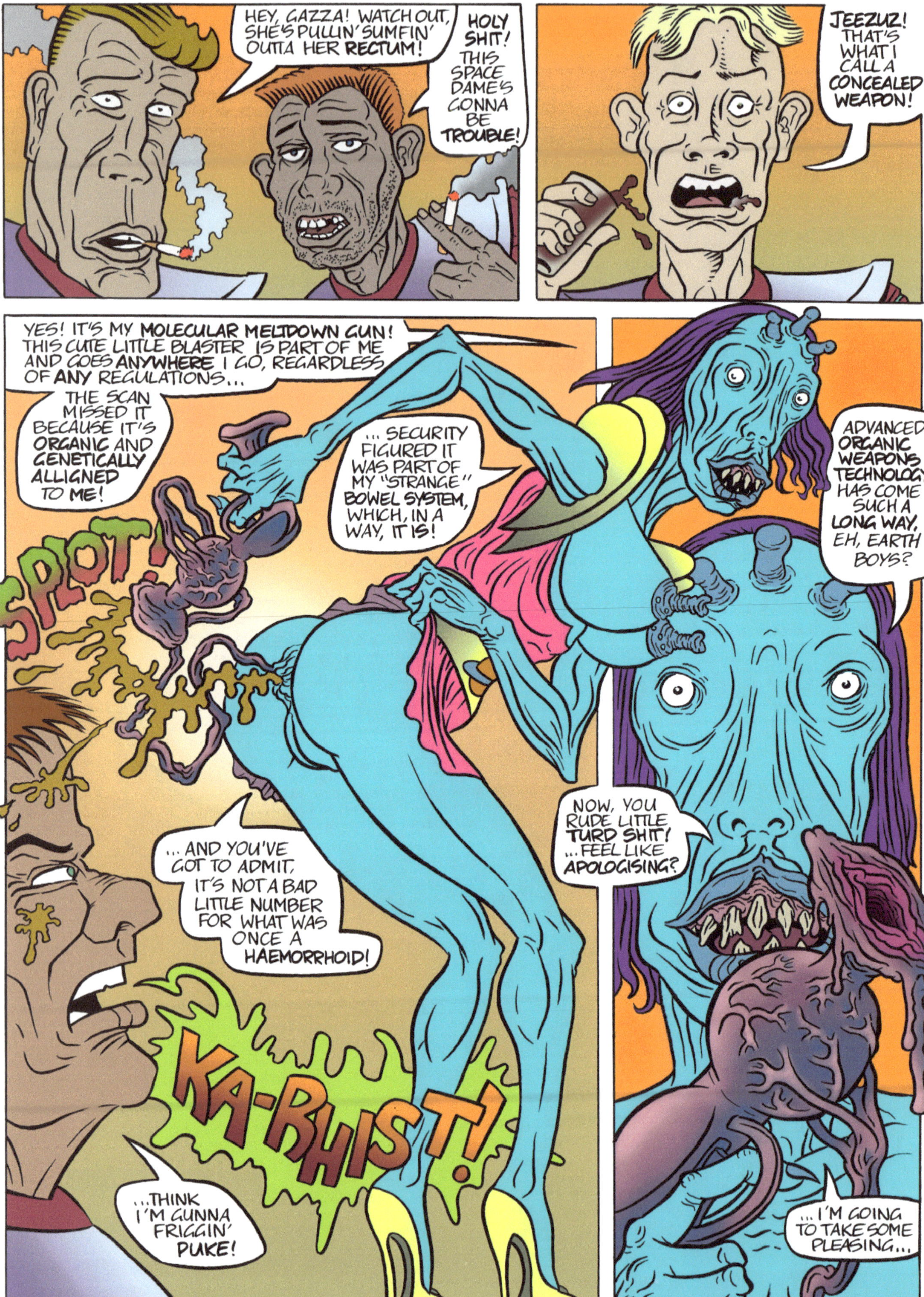

HEY, GAZZA! WATCH OUT, SHE'S PULLIN' SUMFIN' OUTTA HER RECTUM!
HOLY SHIT! THIS SPACE DAME'S GONNA BE TROUBLE!

JEEZUZ! THAT'S WHAT I CALL A CONCEALED WEAPON!

YES! IT'S MY MOLECULAR MELTDOWN GUN! THIS CUTE LITTLE BLASTER IS PART OF ME AND GOES ANYWHERE I GO, REGARDLESS OF ANY REGULATIONS...
THE SCAN MISSED IT BECAUSE IT'S ORGANIC AND GENETICALLY ALLIGNED TO ME!
... SECURITY FIGURED IT WAS PART OF MY "STRANGE" BOWEL SYSTEM, WHICH, IN A WAY, IT IS!
ADVANCED ORGANIC WEAPONS TECHNOLOGY HAS COME SUCH A LONG WAY, EH, EARTH BOYS?
SPLOT!
... AND YOU'VE GOT TO ADMIT, IT'S NOT A BAD LITTLE NUMBER FOR WHAT WAS ONCE A HAEMORRHOID!
NOW, YOU RUDE LITTLE TURD SHIT! ...FEEL LIKE APOLOGISING?
KA-RHIST!
...THINK I'M GUNNA FRIGGIN' PUKE!
...I'M GOING TO TAKE SOME PLEASING...

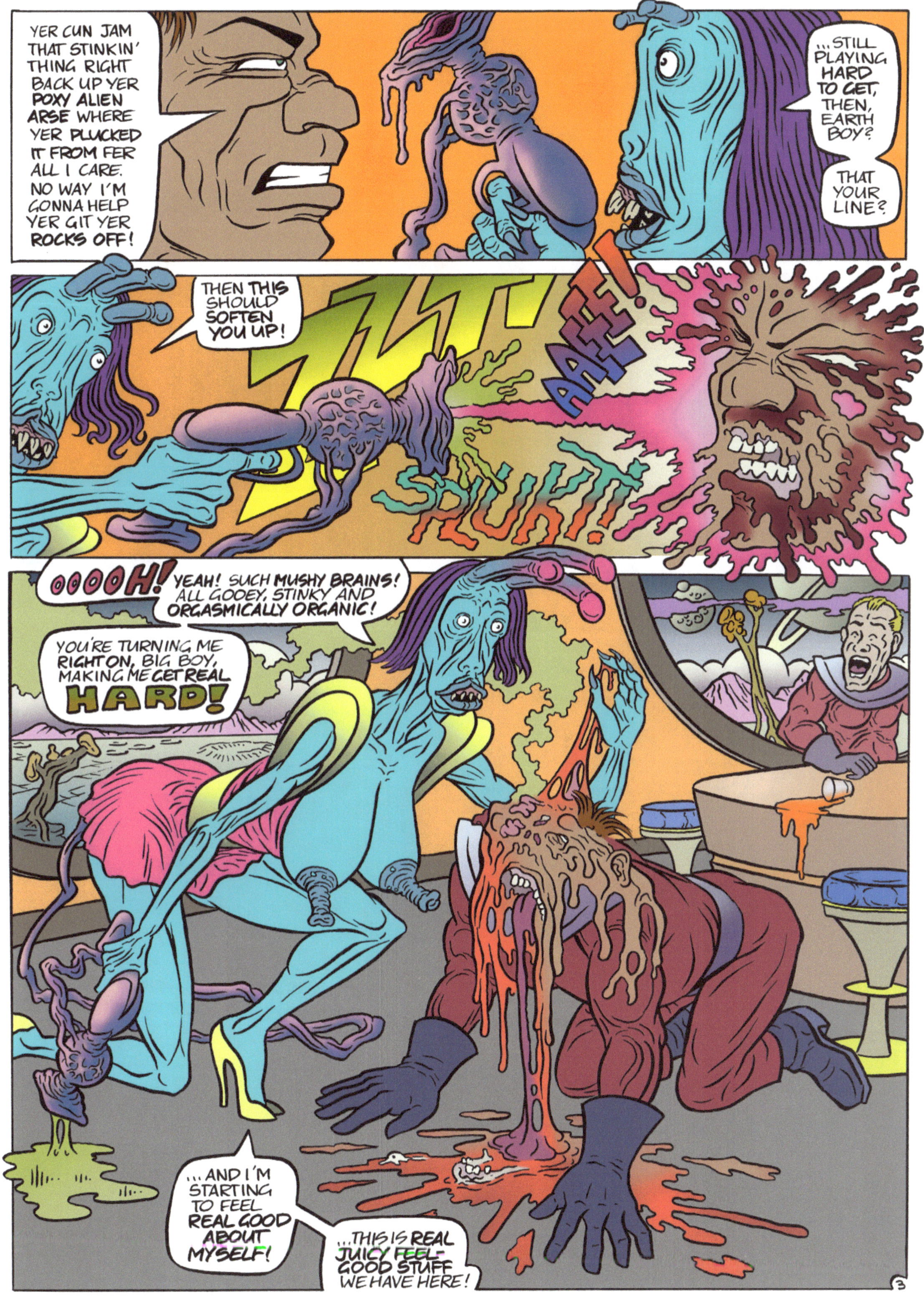

YER CUN JAM THAT STINKIN' THING RIGHT BACK UP YER POXY ALIEN ARSE WHERE YER PLUCKED IT FROM FER ALL I CARE. NO WAY I'M GONNA HELP YER GIT YER ROCKS OFF!
...STILL PLAYING HARD TO GET, THEN, EARTH BOY?
THAT YOUR LINE?
THEN THIS SHOULD SOFTEN YOU UP!
ZZT!
AARGH!
SKRUK!
OOOOH! YEAH! SUCH MUSHY BRAINS! ALL GOOEY, STINKY AND ORGASMICALLY ORGANIC!
YOU'RE TURNING ME RIGHT ON, BIG BOY, MAKING ME GET REAL HARD!
...AND I'M STARTING TO FEEL REAL GOOD ABOUT MYSELF!
...THIS IS REAL JUICY FEEL-GOOD STUFF WE HAVE HERE!

HOW'S THAT FOR A REAL SOGGY MIND FUCK, EH, EARTH BOY?
FUCK YOUR BRAINS RIGHT OUT OF YOUR STUPID HEAD!
ALWAYS KNEW YOU LOT WERE A BUNCH OF FUCKHEADS, HA! HA! HA! HA! HA!
PHLLADH!
SPLOOTSH!
FLUP!
"WHACKY SPAKKI THE SPACE SIREN"
© 1998 S. CARTER
FIN

FROGRE
BY ROSS RADIATION
HEY! WHAT THE..?
RRROOOAAR
HAHAHAHA
HAHAHAHA
OH SHIT!
AAAAAGGHHH!
SOON HE TOO WILL CROAK
HA HA HA
AAAGHHH!
SHHHPPPLLUUUG!
FIN.

If you enjoyed this book by SCAR, have a look at their other titles and please consider writing a review. Thanks!

WEIRD WILD WEST

A New Novel by Carter Rydyr & Ethan Somerville

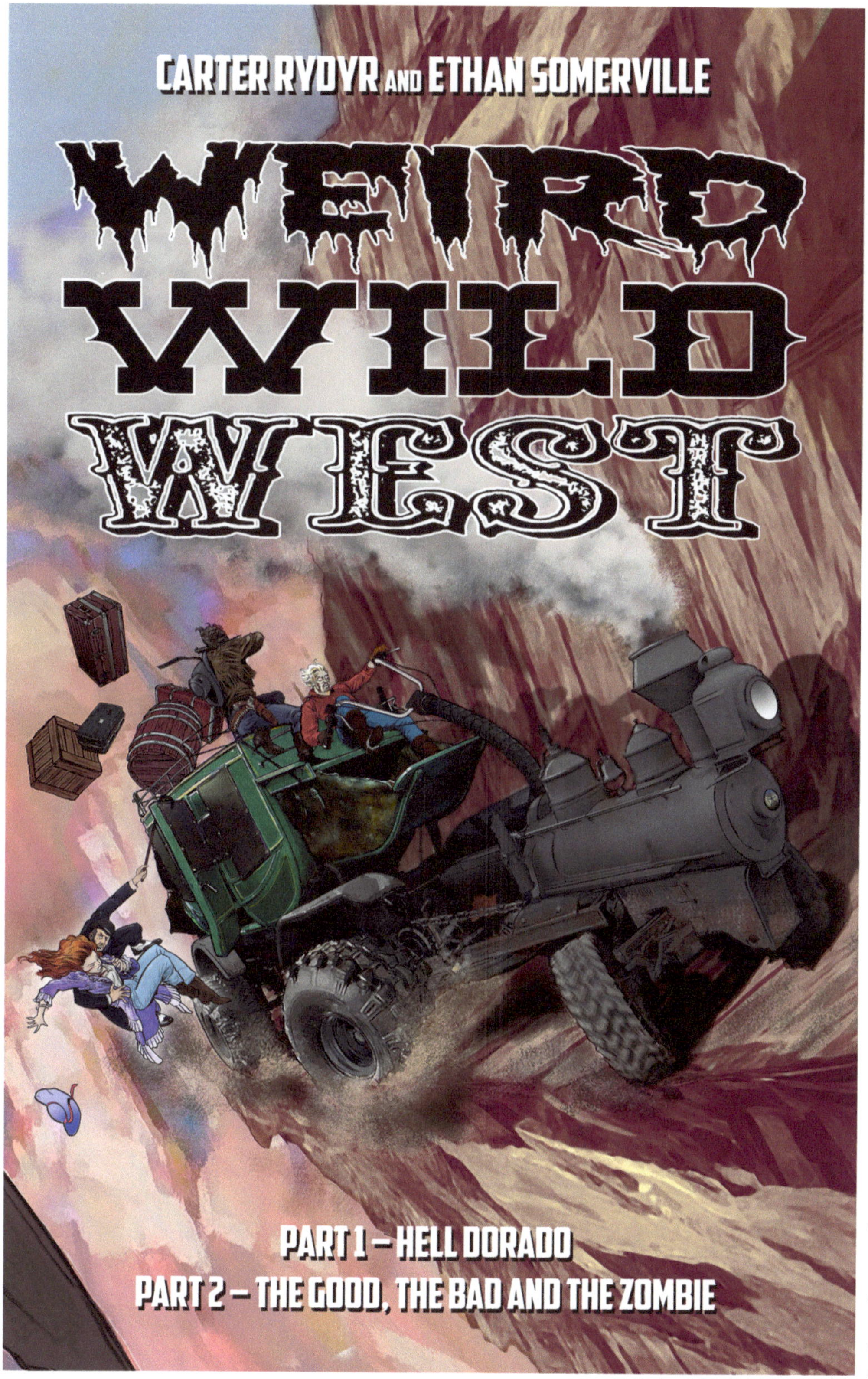

CARTER RYDYR AND **ETHAN SOMERVILLE**

WEIRD WILD WEST

PART 1 – HELL DORADO

PART 2 – THE GOOD, THE BAD AND THE ZOMBIE

Imagine a wild west that isn't just full of cowboys and outlaws, saloon girls and gamblers. Imagine a wild west that isn't just cacti, tumbleweeds and rolling desert as far as the eye can see. Imagine a wild west of mechanical horses, mutant killer plants, flying dinosaurs, headless indians and fearsome zombie gunslingers hell-bent on revenge.

Imagine the Weird Wild West.

Six colourful characters, some not entirely human, embark on a perilous journey south from Sunbleached Plains to Kellyville. A dapper dentist, a southern belle, a wealthy madam, a retired banker turned gambler, an orphaned boy and a travelling body-parts salesman all trade their various stories to pass the time.

Driving the carriage is one Zeke "the Freak" Sarandon, a retired soldier with more than one strange, nervous habit. Although he is an experienced traveller, and the only one insane enough to take the most direct route south, even he cannot prevent his passengers from each meeting their grisly demise, one by one.

Hot on the trail of the coach, astride an ancient mechanical horse blowing sparks and belching out toxic clouds of smoke, is a zombie gunslinger, the risen corpse of a murdered prospector.

For on the carriage is the one who killed him, and he must have his horrible, bloody revenge.

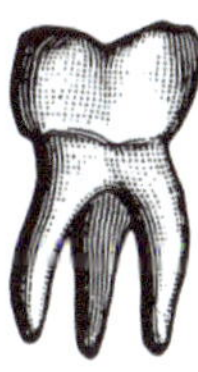

Bizarro Pulp Press

an imprint of JournalStone Publishing.

Published 2018

ISBN: 978-1-947654-40-2

MORE BOOKS BY S.C.A.R.

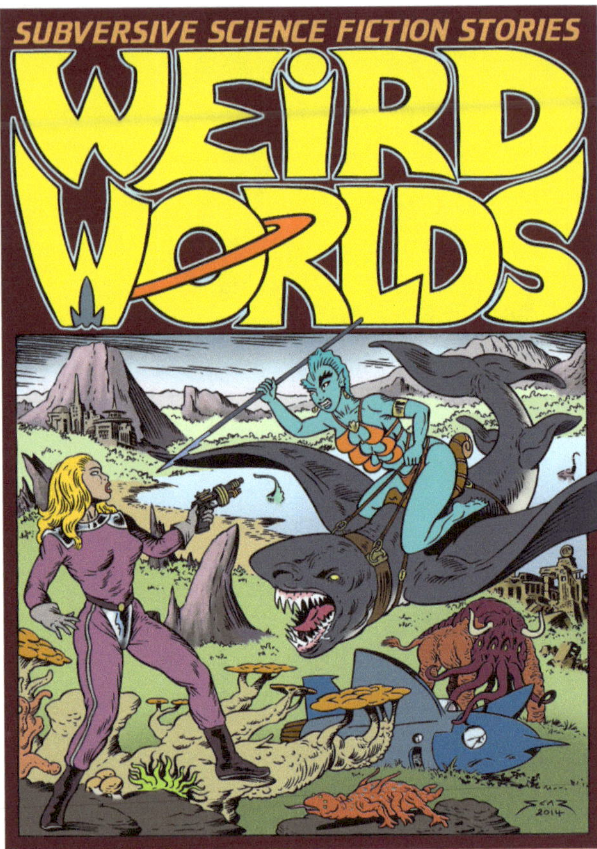

Savage Bitch: ISBN 978-0987622907
Phantastique: ISBN 978-0987622938

Weird Worlds: ISBN 978-0987622914
Fantastique: ISBN 978-0987622921

www.weirdwildart.com

MORE BOOKS BY S.C.A.R.

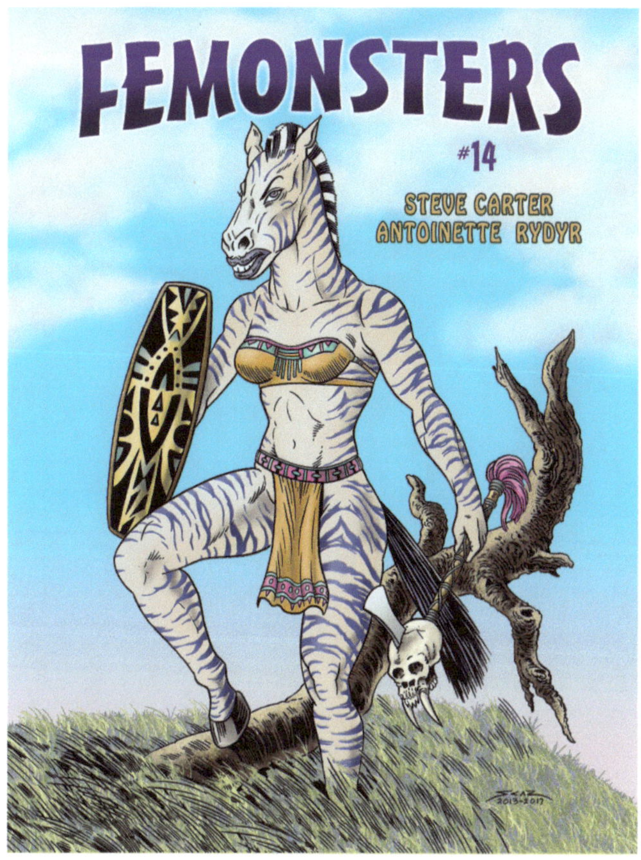

Femonsters #14: ISBN 978-0987622969
Bestiary of Monstruum: ISBN 978-0987622945

New World Disorder: ISBN 978-0987622976
Weird Sex Fantasy: ISBN 978-0987622952

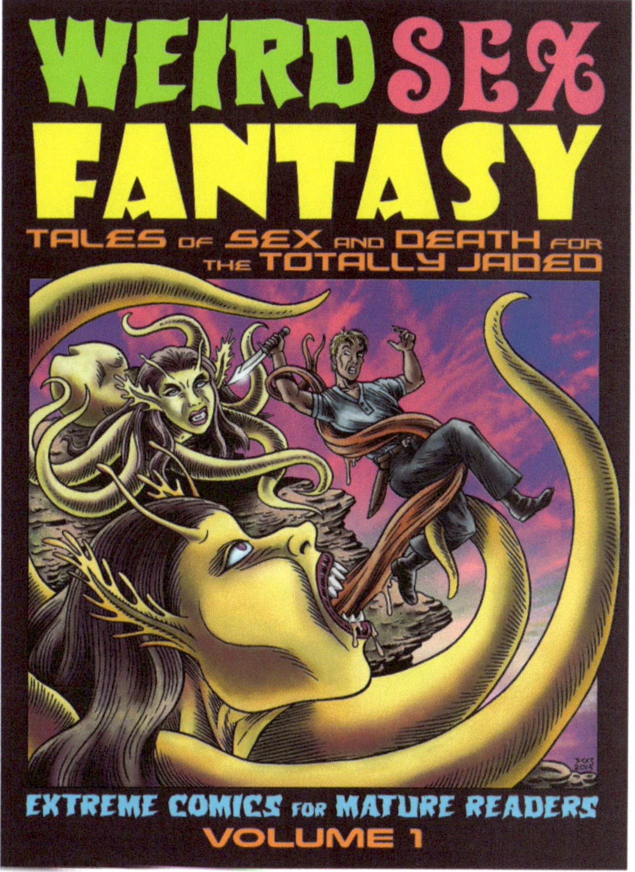

www.weirdwildart.com

www.ingramcontent.com/pod-product-compliance
Lightning Source LLC
Chambersburg PA
CBHW042138120726
47911CB00022B/115